PROTECTING KIMBER

TEAM ATLAS

LYONS TACTICAL INVESTIGATIONS
BOOK 1

LC TAYLOR

Cover designed by Taylored Designs

LC Taylor

www.AuthorLCTaylor.com

First Printing: March 2020

Behind the Badge Press

www.BehindtheBadgePress.com

PROLOGUE

KIMBER WAITED until the door was closed before sitting back on her bed. Her life had become a shit show of epic proportions, and she wasn't sure she wanted to salvage it as it was. The label had ruined what she had planned for her music career when she first started, and now she had a stalker. Life couldn't get any worse, *right*? The fear, it could be, was precisely why going home felt right.

She slipped her cell phone off the table and punched the label manager's contact. This phone call would not go over well, but Kimber didn't care—she needed this desperately. Burnout was a real thing, and she was near combustion.

"Kimber, to what do I owe this Saturday afternoon call?"

"Bryce, look." Kimber sighed. "You won't like this, but it is what it is. I need a break. I want a few months to get my head on straight."

"Seriously, Kimber?" Bryce growled. "Right now?"

"Yes. Right now. If you want that record, you'll give it to me. I'm going home for a little while to recharge. It's the perfect time because my brother needs my help and I need a break. If you don't give this to me, I'll walk away, and there will be no more Stormer Hart."

Kimber had given serious thought over the last few weeks about leaving it all behind—the wigs, the makeup… it was getting old. Then the shit with the letters and mysterious gifts started showing up, and it was the icing on the bullshit cake called her life.

"If you do this, promise to write some new music while you're in bumfuck Egypt. And when you come back, it will be balls to the wall in the studio. And I'll work on a new tour schedule for the upcoming year while you're gone."

"Fine. But I get the final say so on the tour." Kimber hated his demands, but she needed this, and if agreeing to his ridiculous demands meant she got a few months of doing nothing but being Kimber Storm, then she'd do it. "I'll send you the details of my hiatus."

Kimber hung up and leaned back in the chair, relieved the call had gone so quickly. The hard one was next. Convincing Jaxson, her overprotective brother, that she was fine and just needed a vacation, would be tricky. He never bought her bullshit or fell for her lies. So, this was going to be a hard sell.

Glancing at the time, she hoped he could talk. There was no telling if he was out on a mission or back at the base in Afghanistan. Keying up his icon, Kimber pressed the talk button. She half-wished he wouldn't answer so she could avoid it.

"How's my rockstar sister?"

Kimber laughed at him. Jaxson didn't share who she really was with his team. As far as they were concerned, she was just another musician in Nashville, trying to hit it big one day. He'd learned the hard way early on people wanted to be his friend because of her, his famous sister. Plus, he didn't want any of the bad guys he was hunting to have something to use against him.

"Fine… how about you? Gotten any sand in your shorts lately?"

Jaxson groaned. "I fucked up telling you that story because you never let me live it down."

"What? It was funny."

"You wouldn't have thought so if it'd been your ass covered in sand fleas. Seriously, though, Songbird. What's with the random call on a…" Jaxson paused. "Saturday afternoon."

"Well… big brother of mine, I have a proposition for you. I am taking a little hiatus and want to help you get the old house in tiptop shape. I'll stay there and deal with contractors. That way, the house will be ready when you finally make it home."

Kimber bit her lip and held her breath, praying he wouldn't start asking twenty questions. If there was one thing she couldn't do, it was lying to him.

"A hiatus? Why? Is something wrong, Kimber?"

She closed her eyes and counted to ten, willing herself not to crack as she uttered the semi-lie to her brother.

"No. I'm just exhausted. The label wants new songs, and I'm burned out. I've convinced Bryce to give me some time to figure out things, then I'll hit the ground running when I get back."

"I've never liked that dick. You sure there's nothing else?"

"I promise." She swallowed down the guilt of lying to him by omission. "I need a few months to recharge."

There was a long pause, and Kimber wondered if he was about to let his investigative nature take over and grill her.

"Okay. It would help me if someone were there… but only if you're sure."

"Of course, I'm sure. I need this. You need this."

"You know, if I wanted to deal with my buddies going nuts over you, I'd tell them who I was *really* related to and how a rockstar was going to be getting my house ready. But then I'd be opening a can of worms I don't want or need."

"You're stupid." Kimber laughed. "I can't wait for you to come home, Jax. I've missed you."

"I know, kid. I know. I've missed it so much. But soon, I'll be there, and you won't be able to get rid of me. Speaking of time, how's Sparks been working out?"

"Henley is great. He and Avery are together, so I guess I'm stuck with him."

"How about that?" Jaxson chuckled. "Good for him. He's a good guy." A commotion in the background made Jaxson cuss. "Shit, I gotta run, Kimber. I'll send the realtor an email, letting her know you're coming. She can get you the keys. Love you, Kim."

Kimber hung up and blew out a sigh of relief. For the first time in a long time, she could breathe without feeling caged in. Returning home would do her heart and soul some good.

And maybe... just maybe, she'd figure out who she was again.

***

JAXSON CALLED Henley as soon as they'd gotten back to base. Kimber could keep nothing from him, and though she hadn't told him an outright lie, she hadn't been telling the whole truth, either. Henley wouldn't tell him everything that he expected. He was happy to have helped find her someone trustworthy to watch her back. Henley only shared that there were some things that had happened recently, that she was stressed out about it, and that she was taking time off. Jaxson had to respect the man's loyalty to his sister. Her last head of security certainly hadn't known what the word meant.

Tapping his fingers across the folding table, he made a decision, one he knew Kimber would hate if she ever found out. But she was the only family he had left, and he would worry about her while stuck in the sandbox and unable to protect her. Flicking on his phone, he called the one person he could trust to watch her back. If Kimber found out about it, he'd deal with the fallout later.

She wasn't the only one who could omit important information. Hell, as a member of Delta Force, he knew how to do things without being noticed. It was time to use his skills to ensure his sister was safe. The familiar voice answered the phone, making him smile.

"I need a favor."

CHAPTER
ONE

Kimber stared out over the weathered railing and sighed. The weather was cooling, giving way to the fall temps that were not too far off. This was precisely what she needed, even if her bandmates and best friend disagreed with her. They thought she was running instead of dealing with the issue head-on, and maybe she was, but her life in Nashville had slowly started to chip away at her soul. Yeah, she had more money than she knew what to do with, but what had her success cost her? She'd been here for two weeks and already felt lighter. That said something.

Setting the steaming cup of coffee on the ledge, she braced her hands against the splitting wood and glanced around. This place held a lot of memories for her, both good and bad. When she learned it had been left to her and her brother, her heart danced wildly inside her chest with the forgotten life she led before becoming Stormer Hart. Losing the only person who'd been there for them was hard—almost as hard as losing their parents when they were younger. Their Aunt Maggie had been the glue that held them together when their world crashed down on them. They had been happy, and when she got her break in Nashville, she thought the world was finally righting the wrongs she and her brother had faced. Then Maggie died, leaving her memories and a house that had seen better days.

She hadn't left the house much since arriving in Alabama—partly because she was afraid of her stalker finding her. The other had to do with facing people from her past. Growing up here, Kimber was mostly a loner. Before middle school, Jaxson had been her only friend outside of the house… until Avery, who she met freshman year of high school. Her other best friend from high school still lived here. The same friend she and Avery hadn't talked to since hitting it big in Nashville. It wasn't on purpose, but months of not talking turned into years, and before either of them had realized it, they'd lost contact with Sophie.

Jaxson didn't want to sell it, saying he wanted something to come home to when his time in the Army was done, and based on the last few phone calls, that would be awhile. Army was Jaxson's life. Like she'd clung to music as a refuge, he had devoted his life to the military. She was proud of him, even though she missed him like crazy.

A knock echoed through the empty house, pulling her attention from her thoughts. Grabbing the nearly empty mug, she followed through the kitchen toward the front door. She wasn't expecting the contractor this early, but maybe he decided to come sooner. Glancing down at her attire, Kimber winced. A well-worn t-shirt covered her Nike shorts, and her mousy brown hair was piled up on her head in a messy bun. Another loud rap against the wooden barrier between her and the unknown guest made her jump.

"Hang on a second," she practically growled in irritation. Pushing aside her concern about her appearance, she jerked open the door. "You're ea—" Her words died on her tongue when her eyes connected with the stranger standing on her front porch. She had to crane her neck up to see his face, and when she did, her gaze locked on the deepest chestnut eyes she'd ever seen. He was well over six feet tall with the body of a man who hit the gym daily.

"Are you Kimber Storm?" His deep voice sent a thrill of shivers down her spine.

"Um… Y-Yes," she stuttered out her reply. The slight quirk of his lips made her blush in embarrassment. "Sorry… I wasn't expecting you until ten."

"Ah, I think you have me confused with someone else. I'm a friend of Jaxson's. From your reaction, I'm assuming he failed to mention to you that he said I could stay here while my place is being built."

"Excuse me?" Kimber stepped back, thrown for a loop at his words. "My brother Jaxson? Jaxson Storm?"

"Yeah. He and I served together. I'm Rory Maverick."

He thrust his hand out toward her and grinned. Still confused about why her brother wouldn't have called her and told her that a friend was coming to stay at the house, Kimber reluctantly took his hand. A warmth spread through her body, nearly knocking her off her feet and onto her ass. Rory must have felt it, too, because he jerked his arm away and wiped his palm down his jeans.

"I'm not sure what's going on. Do you have an ID or something? I mean… how do I know you are who you say you are?" Kimber glanced around him, scanning the yard. What if the man stalking her in Nashville had found her, and she was about to let him into her home? Granted, something in her gut told her she had nothing to worry about with the hunk of a man standing in front of her.

"He hoped you'd question me." Rory narrowed his gaze at her. "Hang on. Let me call him quick."

"Call him? My brother is not someone you can reach with the flick of a button."

The sound of her brother's voice filled the morning air, irritating her even more since she couldn't get him on a dime notice like the sexy stranger had. Rory explained his situation, making her brother laugh.

"Songbird, are you giving my boy Rory a hard time?"

"Jaxson, what the hell is going on? Your *boy* claims you told him he could stay here."

"Yeah, I forgot. I told him he could crash there before you called me. Look, Kimber, it's a big house, and honestly, I'd feel better if Rory was there to deal with the construction crew." He cleared his throat, "And before you rip me a new one, think about it, Sis. You said you needed a break. You can do that by letting Rory deal with the contractor. It will help him not to have to worry about finding a place to stay while his house is being built. Then you can focus on whatever it is you came home for. I know you want to smash my balls right now, but please, Kimber… do this for me. He's my best friend, and it will ease my worry about you while I'm stuck here for a few more weeks."

Kimber made eye contact with Rory. "Can you give me a minute?" She snatched the device from his hand, stepped inside, and slammed the door closed. If Jaxson were here, she'd have already throat-punched him.

"Jaxson, how am I supposed to have any *privacy* with a stranger in the house? Is this some kind of sick joke? Like… is your BFF some kind of super fan?"

"He has no idea who you are other than being my sister and a musician in Nashville. I've kept it that way for a couple of reasons, Sis. First and foremost, the bad guys knowing who my sister is would have put both of us at risk with what I do for the

Army—that's not a risk I am willing to gamble with. And second, I didn't want people to befriend me because my sister is a superstar. As far as Rory is concerned, you're a musician who makes decent money off your music while trying to become famous. I've never told him differently despite him being my best friend, which is probably shitty on my part. Fuck, I'll have a lot of explaining to do when and if you tell him. That's your choice to make, not mine. Now… let me talk to him so I can threaten him like a proper big brother should."

Kimber pinched her nose and sighed. "I swear if this blows up, I'm blaming you. And threaten him? Seriously, Jaxson, the last thing you need to worry about is me falling for your *boy*." She jerked the door back open and forced a smile. "Here." She thrust her phone back toward him. "My *brother* wants to speak to you. He has some misguided alpha brother bullshit idea that he needs *to threaten* you. Not that he needs to worry about anything happening between us because I don't want you here, anyway."

Kimber turned on her heel and stomped back inside like a toddler. So much for being alone to figure out who she was. Peace and quiet would be a distant memory with her *new* house-guest, who stood on the other side of the door. If she didn't love her brother, she'd fly across the ocean and slap the ever-loving shit out of him for this. How in the hell was she supposed to have solitude with that… that *man* on her front porch?

Her brother was up to something; she knew there was an ulterior motive for his *sudden* presence. But what, Kimber had no clue, nor would she get out of her brother any time soon. Whatever his agenda for sending Rory to live here, Kimber just hoped it didn't blow up in their faces. The last thing she needed was to call attention to her whereabouts.

CHAPTER
TWO

HOLY SHIT.

Rory wasn't prepared for the vibrant energy that greeted him at the door. The pictures he had seen during his time serving with Jaxson hadn't done justice to the fiery sprite who now stood before him. Standing just under his chin, she boasted curves that seemed to defy the laws of physics, a captivating silhouette that commanded attention. Her brown hair, a tempting tangle of chocolate and chestnut, was piled high on her head, like a playfully rebellious crown. Wisps of hair escaped the tousled mound, teasingly framing her face with a flirtatious style that made him pause.

Rory forced himself to maintain eye contact, a feat made challenging by the bare legs that peeked out from beneath a threadbare t-shirt, stopping mid-thigh. His internal monologue screamed at him to focus on her eyes, to resist the allure of what lay beyond. The last thing he needed was to entertain the explicit thoughts racing through his mind about his best friend's sister. Jaxson's disapproving glare loomed in the back of his mind, a stark reminder that indulging in any dirty thoughts about his baby sister would undoubtedly lead to consequences.

Rory tried to suppress the unbidden thoughts that continued to dance through his mind, focusing on the conversation at hand. Little did he know that the unexpected encounter would set off a series of events that would test the limits of loyalty, desire, and the complex dynamics that existed between friends and the tempting forbidden.

He stifled a chuckle when she snatched his phone from his hand and slammed the door on him. Amusement danced in Rory's eyes as he imagined the scene unfolding on the other side. Kimber, a force to be reckoned with, was likely letting loose a barrage of words that matched her fiery personality. He pictured Jaxson, his buddy, receiving an earful of Kimber's unfiltered opinions, and a smirk tugged at his lips at the mental image.

The door jerked open abruptly, and Kimber emerged with a glare that could have frozen hell itself. The intensity of her gaze made Rory momentarily forget the lightheartedness of the situation. Whatever had transpired behind closed doors had left an indelible mark on Kimber's mood. Rory, sensing a shift in the atmosphere, replaced his grin with a more composed expression.

He met Kimber's piercing gaze with an air of readiness, bracing himself for whatever fallout might come his way.

"Here." She thrust her phone back toward him. "My *brother* wants to threaten you. Not that he needs to worry about anything because I don't want you here, anyway."

Rory watched as she sashayed away from him. "Damn, brother, you didn't tell me your sister was a ball buster."

"Yeah, well, I couldn't very well tell her the real reason you were there. She'd have a shit fit for sure."

Rory tore his gaze away from the empty doorway and grunted. "I still don't understand why you need me to watch her."

"I know my sister. She's not telling me something—what I don't know. But with me across the pond, I'll feel better knowing someone's got her six while I can't."

Rory leaned against the wall, phone pressed to his ear, absorbing the weight of Jaxson's concern. He could practically sense the miles between them, the distance amplifying the worry in Jaxson's voice. The responsibility of watching over Kimber, a task that Rory hadn't expected, settled on his shoulders.

"Fine, but when she discovers the truth, remind me to say I told you so."

A hearty laugh echoed through the phone, breaking the tension. Rory couldn't help but appreciate the humor in Jaxson's words. The timing of his best friend's call, despite the unexpected twist in responsibilities, couldn't have been more opportune. After a year spent babysitting Hollywood's spoiled starlets, the move to Alabama had been a breath of fresh air for Rory. He missed the Army, especially his team and the camaraderie that came with it.

A twinge in his knee served as a constant reminder of a mission gone awry, forcing him to make a tough choice—retire or accept a desk job. Rory, with his aversion to confinement, chose the former. Los Angeles had been a brief detour, a stint as a bodyguard, a role that chafed against his principles. Protecting those he loathed became a test of his patience, and he yearned for a more meaningful role in civilian life. When Rory called, then subsequently put him in touch with Ares Lyons, an acquaintance from joint operations their team had done with the Navy, he was more than happy to help Jaxson.

Ares offered him a lifeline, specifically a job in his stateside security business. Lyons Tactical Investigation, or LTI, operated two segments of security—Personal Protection and Investigations for US-based clients, while Team Obsidian deals with international threats. The difference between what Ares was offering and what he did in Hollywood was they worked for regular people, not just the rich and entitled. Little did he know that the journey ahead would unveil challenges that tested not only his protective instincts but also the depths of loyalty and unforeseen connections that awaited him in the heart of Alabama.

Kimber, whether aware or oblivious, had unwittingly become Rory's first mission in his new role. Only a select few knew his true purpose—himself, his boss, Atlas, and, of course, Jaxson. To Kimber, he was just a helpful friend assisting with renovations, settling into a new job at Lyons Tactical Innovations (LTI), and needing a place to stay during the transition. Granted, he didn't need a place to stay, seeing as Lyons Tactical was housed on several acres of land that offered a dorm of sorts to the men he employed. He had an apartment there but gathered enough stuff to bring to her place. He did need time to acclimate to the area. Plus, she'd be bound to see his weapons at some point, so the shred of truth about his employer made keeping his cover intact easier. This way, when she saw the small armory of weapons Ares fitted him with, she wouldn't be suspicious.

"Look, my sister is all I have left, Rory. I can't lose her, and I know deep down something is wrong. For her to just up and leave Nashville like she did is telling. Maybe she'll open up to you as a *friend*."

Rory didn't miss him stressing the word *friend*. "Don't worry, Jaxson. She's a job, not my next hookup. Besides, I'd never cross a line with a charge."

"Fine. Just don't forget who her brother is." He laughed, making Rory shake his head.

"Oh, I'm well aware of who her brother is, *Ice*." Jaxson earned his nickname for turning off all emotions when dealing with the enemy. He was like an Ice Storm, freezing them out until they finally begged for mercy. "Relax. You keep yourself safe over there, and I'll keep her safe here. Promise, Brother. I have her six."

"Alright, Maverick. I trust you with her life. Until Tomorrow."

"Stay safe, Ice."

Pocketing his phone, Rory turned and jogged back to his SUV. Another perk of working with Ares Lyons was a company car. The decked-out Ford Expedition came with every bell and whistle possible, including blacked-out windows coated in bullet-resistant film. Ares had a silent investor, one Rory suspected was embedded deep in the government. He didn't offer up the information, and Rory didn't ask. Frankly, he didn't care.

Grabbing the duffle bag and gun case from the backseat, Rory locked the truck and headed back inside. He kicked the door shut and set his things down in the foyer. The house had great bones, but it was apparent it hadn't been lived in for a while.

"Shit." He heard Kimber's voice from the kitchen.

Making his way into the room, he skidded to an abrupt stop when his eyes landed on her backside. She was bent over, picking up mirrored shards off the ground. Snapping out of his momentary state of ogling her pert ass, he realized she was standing barefoot, surrounded by the remains of what used to be a glass.

"Whoa, firecracker," Rory exclaimed, his protective instincts kicking in. Without hesitation, he rushed forward, spun her around, and gripped her hips as he effortlessly lifted her into his arms. "You're going to get yourself cut."

"What the fuck?" The defiant protest escaped her lips. "Put me down, you big oaf." She twisted within his hold, attempting to free herself, but Rory held firm to ensure her safety.

"Don't think so. You're not wearing any shoes," Rory remarked with a hint of amusement as he gently plopped her down on the counter. "Sit tight while I clean this up. Where's the broom?"

"In there." Kimber pointed to a small pantry door, her frustration palpable.

Turning around, he expected to find Kimber off the counter, but she was still seated, her expression a mix of annoyance and discomfort. Confusion etched his features as he was about to ask her what had happened when his gaze fell upon the crimson towel pressed against her foot.

"Shit… you cut yourself," Rory muttered, a sudden urgency in his voice. He rushed to stand in front of her, gently lifting her foot to inspect the injury. "Why didn't you say something, Kimber?"

"I didn't realize the glass hit my foot."

There was a small cut across her shin. It was pretty superficial, but it bled like a stuck pig. Rory grabbed a handful of paper towels and replaced the soaked ones with the new ones. "Where's the first aid kit?"

"In the half-bath in the hallway under the sink."

"Sit tight. I'll be right back."

The unexpected turn of events left Rory perplexed. How in the hell had Kimber managed to get hurt within the first thirty minutes of his presence? A sense of foreboding crept into his thoughts, and he silently prayed this incident wasn't an ominous prelude to the days ahead. The last thing he wanted was to make that dreaded call to Jaxson, confessing that his sister had suffered an injury under Rory's watch. After a quick mental inventory of the situation, Rory shook off the unsettling feeling and refocused on the task at hand, hurrying out of the room to retrieve the first aid kit.

"Not sure if this old thing will have what we need." He set it down on the counter beside her and grabbed her leg. Pressing her foot into his chest, he wiped away the slow trickle of blood from her skin. He opened an antiseptic wipe and glanced up at Kimber. "This might burn." He dabbed the skin lightly, not wanting to hurt her. She winced at his touch.

"Sorry, I knew it would sting, but it still shocked me."

Rory blew a stream of hot breath across her skin, trying to tamper the burning sensation she was likely feeling. The warmth, a stark contrast to the discomfort she was likely experiencing, was a slight gesture to ease the burning sensation caused by the cut. His focus unwavering, Rory reached into the box, retrieving a packet of ointment with practiced efficiency. Tossing the trash aside, he tugged out a band-aid and quickly covered the damaged flesh. As he finished applying the band-aid, Rory cast a glance at Kimber, his eyes meeting hers with an unspoken acknowledgment of the shared moment.

"There. Good as new." He kept his hand on her leg longer than he should have.

Kimber must have felt the strange energy coursing between them, because she jerked her leg out of his grasp and slid off the counter.

"Thanks for helping me. I'll show you where you'll be sleeping… unless you've decided to stay in town."

"Nah, promised your brother I'd look after the place."

"Right." She turned and glanced over her shoulder. "Follow me, then."

He couldn't help but watch as her bare legs gracefully limped out of the kitchen, leaving him in a reflective state, wondering why she had the power to tie him up in knots. He couldn't fuck up this assignment because his ward was hot as fuck. She was *off-limits* in more ways than one. He chalked the attraction up to her being normal and not one of the starlets he'd been surrounded by for the last twelve months. Once he got settled, he'd go out and find a woman to wet his dick and forget all about the blue-eyed vixen who was a walking death trap. Getting caught up in that trap would mean the end of his new job *and* his friendship with her brother.

When he caught up to Kimber, she was almost at the top of the steps. Rory grabbed his bag and weapons and hurried up behind her. She looked over her shoulder.

"What exactly are you doing here in Copper Springs?"

"Working for Lyons Tactical Investigations."

She paused, making him walk into her. "Shit." He gripped her shoulders to keep her from pitching forward. "Sorry, wasn't expecting you to stop."

"My fault. This is you." She pushed open a door and stepped aside. "The other rooms are empty right now. My room is across the hall, and unfortunately, we have to share the bathroom right there." She pointed to a door at the end of the hallway. "The master bedroom is torn apart right now. According to the realtor, the room's floor was rotted out and unlivable, which means the master bathroom is also out of order. Towels are in the closet beside the bathroom, and the laundry room is downstairs in the mudroom at the rear of the house." She watched as he stepped inside the decent-sized room and dropped his things.

Rory glanced around the room and smiled. "This is nice. I can't say that I see Jaxson living in a house this big."

"Me, either, but it was our Aunt Maggie's house and where we grew up. He couldn't let it go, and honestly, neither could I.

Frankly, I'm glad he kept it. I needed somewhere to escape, and this was the only place I wanted to come."

"Why'd you need to get away?" Rory was curious if she'd open up to him. He knew it was a long shot, but he asked anyway. "Your brother said you loved living in Nashville."

She narrowed her gaze at him and sighed. "I do. I just needed a vacation." She straightened her, effectively walling him out. "I've got to get dressed. The contractor will be here soon."

Rory watched as she spun on her heel and stormed into her room. Her door slamming was a clear indicator he had touched a nerve. Shit… finding out what she was hiding, something he was confident she was, would be challenging to get her to confess.

He unpacked his clothes and stowed his things in the closet and dresser, then pushed the gun case under the queen-sized bed and stood. He chuckled, thinking about sleeping in the antique bed. Hell, at six foot three, his feet would likely hang off the end of the brass bedframe, but he'd slept in worse conditions, so he wouldn't be complaining about his current accommodations anytime soon.

Rory left the sanctuary of his room and headed down the stairs. He wanted to check out the property to know what kind of security he needed to get installed. He was about to step outside when Kimber's heels drew his attention to the steps.

She practically floated down the steps wearing jeans molded to her curvy frame, accentuating her perfectly shaped legs encased in pink cowboy boots. The shirt—if he could call it that—was a long-sleeved crop top that hung off one shoulder. Her once messy bun was down and weaved into a side braid that rested against her bare shoulder. His cock pulsed beneath his jeans as he held his gaze on Kimber.

Fuck, he was in trouble.

CHAPTER
THREE

Kimber wanted to convince herself that her brother was innocent, and the enticing man downstairs was nothing more than a bizarre coincidence, but she knew her brother, and Rory, was anything *but* a coincidence. He was a problem.

She knew her brother well, understood the complexities of his life, and sensed Rory's arrival was more than serendipity. The temptation to confront the undeniable truth between Jaxson knowing she wanted to be here, and Rory's arrival clawed at Kimber's thoughts.

Descending the steps, Kimber couldn't escape the palpable tension that hung in the air. As her eyes met Rory's, she couldn't help but notice the subtle yet undeniable reaction he had to her presence. It was a mirror image of the internal struggle she was trying to suppress, his demeanor betraying a magnetic pull that echoed her own conflicted emotions. The unspoken connection between them, like an invisible thread, pulled at the edges of a secret they both held. She wanted to be pissed at his presence, but standing there, caught in a silent exchange, Kimber couldn't ignore the fact that Rory was affected by her in ways that went beyond casual observation. The air seemed charged with a shared awareness, leaving them both navigating the uncharted territory of mutual attraction.

"You okay?" she inquired, a playful yet challenging lift of her brow punctuating the question. The blatant ogling hadn't gone unnoticed by him, and Kimber's gaze held a mixture of curiosity and a hint of amusement, almost daring him to say something. The charged atmosphere lingered.

"Yeah. I'm just gonna walk around outside and see the lay of the land."

She shook her head. "Can't stop being a soldier, can you?" Kimber mumbled under her breath as she folded her arms across her chest. "The contractor should be here soon. Thought you were gonna be his contact man."

As if conjured out of thin air, a knock interrupted their conversation. Rory turned and peeked out the peephole before pulling open the door.

"Can I help you?"

An older man stood on the other side of the open doorway.

"I'm Hal Kitchens. I have an appointment to speak with Kimber Storm."

"That's me." She pushed past Rory to stand in front of him and stuck her hand out. "This is Rory Maverick. He'll be your point man on this project."

"I wasn't aware there was anyone else living here."

Rory bristled behind her. "I'm here now, so I'll be the one you'll deal with."

"Fine by me, meant no harm in my statement. I was a little worried when the realtor told me a single woman lived in this house alone. I have daughters who are probably close to your age, Miss Storm. Wouldn't want them alone in the woods like I thought you were. His being here is a relief."

"I'm fine, I assure you." Kimber turned to Rory. "I'll leave you two to talk. The plans are on the kitchen table. In the meantime, I'm going to grab the mail."

She hurried past the man and descended the weathered boards of the front porch. In the three weeks since returning to Copper Springs, she had confined herself to the property, a blend of fear and a desire to avoid encounters with anyone who might recognize her motivating the self-imposed isolation. Stormer Hart and Kimber Storm existed as two distinct personas shaped by the demands of the record label. Stormer Hart was the fabricated image meticulously crafted to meet the label's expectations. Initially enthralled by the allure of glitz and glamor, she had silenced the tiny voice inside her head and complied with the prescribed look.

HOWEVER, nearly ten years had passed since then, and the novelty of makeup and costumes had worn thin. The truth was, no one would easily recognize her as Stormer Hart. The alter ego sported a short, platinum blonde angled bob, accentuated by the exaggerated makeup adorning her face. If asked to describe her band, she would compare them to a contemporary version of Gem and the Holograms. It wasn't the kind of music she aspired to be known for, but the initial conformity to the label's wishes had relegated her own desires to the background after the first few years.

This break couldn't have come at a more opportune moment, providing Kimber with the clarity she needed to navigate the next steps in her career. At twenty-seven, she found herself at a crossroads, ready to slow down and contemplate the possibility of starting a family. Naturally, this would entail having a special man in her life. In her thoughts, Rory occupied a prominent place, his presence lingering in her mind even as she trekked to the mailbox.

The walk served as a temporary escape from the complicated emotions stirred by Rory's presence at the house. In the span of the last two hours, he had evoked a chaotic response within her, a sensation she was hesitant to confront.

Reaching the mailbox, Kimber pulled open the metal lid and retrieved the stack of mail that had accumulated over the past few days. Although she should have made it a daily routine to clear out the bin, she neglected the task. As she sifted through the familiar mix of junk mail, her hand halted at an envelope addressed to her, devoid of a return address.

"Weird," she murmured to herself, tucking the stack beneath her armpit. With the mysterious piece of mail in hand, Kimber retraced her steps, striding back up the long driveway with a sense of unease about the contents of the unmarked envelope.

She found Mr. Kitchens and Rory standing in the front yard.

"Kimber," Rory called out, beckoning her to them. "Mr. Kitchens said he'll have a crew over to start tomorrow. They're going to start on the master first, then work their way down to the first floor."

"Please, call me Hal. Miss Storm, we'll eventually get to your bedroom and Mr. Maverick's room, but you'll have use of the master by that time."

"Works for me. I'd appreciate it if you left the office downstairs for last and always kept the door closed. It houses several instruments, and I don't need sheetrock dust or chemicals to get onto them accidentally."

"You're a musician?"

Kimber shifted uneasily on her feet. "Um… I write music and play a little."

"I see. I'll be sure to tell the crew your request. If you have any issues, you can contact me or talk to the foreman, Clint Stevens. He'll be the main point of contact day to day. I'll come out periodically to check on the progress. Otherwise, I trust my crew to handle things."

"Sounds good. Rory, I've got to run some errands. You need anything?"

"Hang tight, and I'll drive us into town."

"I can drive myself." Kimber pressed her hands to her hips and narrowed her gaze. "I don't need a babysitter."

"Maybe not, but I need a tour guide. You're from around here, and I'd rather not rely on you to run my errands."

Kimber blushed. "Sorry… Fine. I'll go grab my purse and meet you at the car."

She scampered away and hastily fled indoors. He had a way of unsettling her, causing her to lose her composure. The mere presence of Rory had thrown her into disarray, leaving her questioning how she would function with him around. It had been barely half a day, and she found herself torn between—throttling him or kissing him, neither of which seemed like a wise idea.

Throwing the pile of mail onto the kitchen counter, she swiftly grabbed her purse and phone. The mail could wait; at this moment, her priority was to figure out how to endure a car ride with Rory without subjecting herself to potential embarrassment.

Rory was standing by the blacked-out Expedition when she emerged from the house. He was propped against the front bumper with his arms folded across his massive chest.

"The contractor leave already?"

"Yep." Rory pushed off the truck and tugged open the passenger door.

Kimber struggled to climb in, leading Rory to grip her sides and hoist her into the passenger seat. Kimber let out a squeak but held her tongue as he shut the door and walked around the front end. She was buckling her seatbelt when he climbed in behind the steering wheel.

"Where to first?"

"The grocery store." She smiled. "Head down the driveway and hang a left. We'll go about two miles, then take a right. The grocery store will be on the right. Is Lyons Tactical Investigation in Town?"

"They're on the edge of Copper Springs. I'm pretty sure I passed the supermarket on my way to your house. The building is on about fifteen acres of land. It's pretty cool. I can take you there sometime if you want to see it. Ares, one of the owners, lives on-site. Actually, he and his brothers, Riggs and Atlas, own the business together. Riggs also lives on-site, and Atlas has one more year in the Navy before he joins them."

"Wow, three boys."

"And a sister. Callen owns a dress shop in town."

"Wow, okay. Must be nice to have a big family. What about you? Where is your family? What brought you here, of all places?"

Rory glanced over at her and smiled. "I'm actually a twin."

"No shit?" Kimber's eyebrows hit her hairline. "A twin?"

"Yep… Roslyn lives in Ohio with my parents, who are both teachers. She's dating a teacher my parents set her up with. I suspect I'll be getting a call any day now that she's getting married. She's a clothing designer, small-time but good. As for what brought me here, I needed a change." A strange emotion crossed his features, as if he was remembering something painful.

She wanted to ask about it, but decided against it for now.

Kimber shifted in her seat. "I understand needing a change. Anyone special coming to be with you?"

"Nah. My career in the Army wasn't conducive to relationships. And when I first got out, I was busy babysitting Hollywood's whiney stars. Coming to Alabama was a blessing. I wasn't sure how much longer I could deal with the entitled women I was protecting."

Kimber grunts. "You don't like rich people?"

"Not particularly. The women I guarded threw fits over their coffee being made wrong or took hours to put their makeup on. I can't stand fake women or people. It wasn't the job for me. What about you?"

Kimber bit her tongue. She was the exact kind of person he was talking about---well, minus the coffee tantrums.

"My career doesn't really allow for them, either."

Rory scrunched his brows. "Writing music makes dating hard?"

"Nope." Kimber bit her lip, remembering he had no idea who she was in Nashville. He'd probably hate her if he did. "Unfortunately, the decent guys in Nashville all think women are using them for something, and the ones who don't have that mentality are shit. Besides, trying to make it in the music world leaves little time for dating."

"You don't date?"

Kimber blushed. "No. I don't date."

Rory seemed shocked by her admission. "That's a shame. You're a beautiful woman, Kimber. I'd have thought a man would have snatched you up and put a ring on your finger. Surely, they could lock you down and support your dreams."

She wished that was the case, but the existence of her alter ego imposed restrictions on her ability to get close to men. Unless it was someone the label meticulously vetted and required to sign a nondisclosure agreement, forming genuine connections became a challenging endeavor. While she had experienced intimacy in the past, it had been so long ago, she questioned her ability to navigate such interactions now. For the past six years, her orgasms had been self-induced, and she harbored a secret she was unwilling to share—a recent date involving four double-A batteries and a bottle of wine. It was a detail she certainly wasn't prepared to confess to the infuriating hunk seated beside her.

"You're talking about a unicorn, Rory. They don't exist."

"Or maybe you've been looking in the wrong places."

She realized they'd reached their destination when he killed the engine and climbed out. Rory stood at the front of the SUV, waiting for her to join him. Slowly pushing open the door, she slid down until her feet hit the pavement. Taking a deep breath of the crisp country air, Kimber slowly eased around the truck.

"Let's grab some lunch first." Rory grinned at her. "My stomach is about to eat itself, and if I go into the store like this, we'll wind up with more than we need."

"Lead the way, hungry boy," she said, nodding her head.

"Boy…" Rory paused, casting her a look that nearly melted her panties. "Not sure what you're used to, Kimber, but I'm no boy."

Oh, she was well aware of that. Rory was one hundred percent man. And she was about ready to throw caution to the wind and convince him to have a no-strings relationship. The kind that would mutually benefit them both. He might be staying in Copper Springs, but her stay was temporary for now. A hookup with the *hot* former Delta Force Operator might be just the medicine she needed to forget all about the shitstorm waiting on her in Nashville.

CHAPTER
FOUR

Rory sat on the back steps of the sprawling porch and stared off into the emptiness of the massive property. Nothing but trees and grass as far as the eye could see. He'd come out here many times, trying to tamper his desire for the woman inside. Everything about her drew him in like a moth to a flame—only he wasn't afraid of being burned.

The noise of heavy pounding reminded him they weren't alone. So far, in the ten days he'd been around Kimber, he had seen nothing unusual. He wasn't sure Jaxson's concerns were valid, but being here had been his most straightforward job. Though he was having a tough time thinking of Kimber as a job—and *that* was the problem, which is why he was outside sitting on the steps staring into nothing.

"Hiding from the noise?" Her voice washed over him like warm water, making him shiver.

Craning his head to look back at her, he stifled a groan. She was wearing a sundress that stopped mid-thigh, displaying her beautiful legs.

"Yeah, but I'm not doing a good job of it, seeing as I can still hear them."

"Well, you're gonna love this, then. Apparently, Hal wasn't clear about how things would work when they moved on to the spare rooms. They began moving your things into my bedroom. One of us will have to sleep on the couch because mine has no room…"

"I've slept on worse. A couch will work for me. Wait… they moved my shit?" Rory jumped to his feet and practically knocked Kimber down as he bowled past her. "They better not have fucked with my weapons." He took the steps two at a time until he was standing inside the dismantled room. Clint was coming out of the bathroom.

"Mr. Maverick, I was just about to dismantle your bed. They've already moved the dressers across the hallway. He tipped his head in the direction of Kimber's room.

"If you don't mind… I need to move something out from under the bed." Rory squatted to his knees beside the mattress and tugged out a long metal case. With the handle clutched in his fingers, he stood. "Kimber, if it's alright with you, I'll store this in the master closet. I assume you're done with that room?" He turned to Clint.

"Yep. The master bathroom, closet, and suite are all done. You'll have to use that bathroom from here on out. My guys will be ripping out the old tub in the spare bathroom today."

"Wonderful," Rory growled as he toted the heavy case toward the bedroom. As soon as he stepped through, he jerked to a stop, causing Kimber to slam into his backside.

"What the hell?" she pushed around him and stopped. "Wow."

The room was completely transformed. The once ancient sconces were gone, and instead, recessed lighting lit the room. The once unused fireplace was redone to be open and, well, humongous. Soft gray walls were bare, waiting for a personal touch.

"When did that get in here?" Kimber pointed to the rustic wood king-sized bed frame that occupied most of the room.

"They guys assembled it once the floors were done." Clint's voice carried from the hallway.

And damn, the floors were a work of art themselves, a hardwood that rivaled the rustic wood of the bed. A massive black rug covered a portion of the floor, making Kimber want to lie down on it and roll around.

"If you like this… check out the bathroom. Mr. Storm ensured no expense was spared for the remodel in there."

Rory stifled a laugh when Kimber bounced on her feet and rushed toward the bathroom.

"Holy Shit, Rory. You gotta see this."

He set the case down, strolled toward the open door, and froze. "Jaxson certainly went all out."

The room had been gutted, and an actual work of art was in its place. New countertops were the opposite of what Rory considered the most exquisite shower he'd ever seen. Granted, his idea of a shower was a hose or bucket of water when he was part of Delta Force, but this… he was sure, was beyond anything he'd ever encountered.

"I want to shower first." Kimber clapped her hands. "I can't believe my brother had this put in. He's never struck me as the type to care too much about taking a luxurious shower."

"Miss Storm." A faint voice sounded from downstairs.

Kimber shot Rory a weird look before pushing past him and Clint.

"Whoa. Slow down, Kimber."

He reached out and slowed her descent down the steps. When they reached the bottom, Rory craned and peered around the wall to see one of the workers holding a massive vase filled with red roses.

"Ma'am, these were delivered to you. Hope it was alright that I signed for them."

"It's fine." Kimber smiled as she reached out and grabbed the ostentatious floral arrangement. "Who delivered them?"

"Canes Florist in town."

"Thanks." She spun away from Rory and carried them into the kitchen. Rory watched as she leaned forward, inhaled the sweet scent, and stepped back. "Wonder who on earth would send these to me?"

Rory wondered the same thing. Kimber had indicated she wasn't dating anyone, and those kinds of flowers were usually sent by someone expressing affection. He watched as she pulled the tiny white envelope off the card stand and slipped the card inside out to read. Her face flickered with a weird expression, morphing into one that showed no emotion whatsoever, making Rory wonder what it said.

"Who's it from? A secret admirer?" He chuckled, trying to break the weird silence that had taken over the room. When she didn't answer, Rory stepped forward. "Kimber?"

Jerking at the sound of her name, she crumbled the card and tossed it into the trashcan. "Sorry, I was lost in thought."

"Well... are they from a beau?"

"Told you I don't have one of those. It's from a friend. That's all. I'm going to head into my office for a bit. Call me when you get hungry. Maybe we can go out and grab a bite to eat."

She didn't wait for a response as she disappeared down the hall. The resounding sound of the door slamming told him that whoever sent them wasn't someone she cared to hear from. Waiting to see if she came back out, Rory stood by the trash can. When he was certain she wasn't coming out of her office, he reached in and snatched out the card. He unfurled the cardboard paper and stared down at the two words written in ink.

Miss me?

Rory's hackles rose at the simple statement. Not only were the words odd, but her reaction to them told him something wasn't right. He fished his phone out and did a quick search for the florist's name printed on the back. Dialing the number listed, he waited patiently for someone to answer.

"Cane's Florist, Harper speaking."

"Hi, Harper. My name is Rory Maverick, and I'm wondering if you could help me with a delivery your store just made." He spat out the address and waited.

"Oh, I see those were just dropped off. Was there a problem with the delivery?"

"Actually, I am trying to see who sent them. There wasn't a name on the card, but it looked handwritten."

"According to the order, it was a call-in. Most likely, one of the designers wrote the message for the customer. That happens pretty often."

"I see. Any chance you can tell me who called it in?"

"Let me check." He could hear her clicking keys as she mumbled to herself. "Weird. It was paid with a gift card, but there isn't a name associated with the order. I hope everything was okay with the flowers."

"They were fine. Thank you for checking."

He disconnected the call and pocketed his phone. Until now, he hadn't really seen a need to put up cameras, but something in his gut wasn't sitting right with this. He padded his way down the hallway and paused outside Kimber's office door.

He'd heard her play several times over the last few weeks, but until this time, the music she tapped out on the piano sounded... sad. Pushing open the door, he quietly stepped inside. She was so completely lost in the notes she tapped out, she didn't notice him.

"You're really good." He watched as she turned to face him, her fingers hovering over the keys. "I'm surprised you don't have a record deal of your own."

She stiffened but shook it off quickly, but not before he saw it.

"Thanks, but I just do what I'm told and make music." She pulled the lid over the ivory and stood. "You hungry? I'm starving."

She started toward him, and for some reason, he decided the skirt around his attraction was stupid. Rory wrapped his fingers around her arm and pulled her against his body. Her curvy frame fit perfectly against his, and when he threaded his fingers through her silky strands, he tugged her lips against his. When she moaned against his mouth, he knew he'd made the right decision. The world around them faded into insignificance as the magnetic pull between their lips drew them closer. The music room, once filled only with the sounds of her instruments, now bore witness to the delicate overture of something blooming between them. This attraction was a force Rory didn't think he could fight, nor did he want to.

When he finally pulled back, her eyes were unfocused, and her lips were swollen from the kiss he'd taken without any ounce of regret.

"I've wanted to kiss you from the moment you opened the door, Kimber."

She blinked, clearing the haze of desire that was polluting the pools of blue staring at him. "I… Rory," she whispered his name, and at first, he thought she might regret the kiss, but when she rose on her tiptoes and covered his mouth again, all rational thought left his brain.

Hoisting her body up, he spun them so her back was against the keys he'd somehow closed first. Her fingers speared his hair as he licked and sucked at the smooth flesh of her neck. Kimber rubbed her core against the bulge in his pants, making his dick jerk with need.

"Please Rory…" Kimber's breathless plea made him crazy with desire.

Not stopping to think about the repercussions or the fact his best friend—her brother—would probably put a bullet between his eyes, Rory slipped his hand beneath her dress and pressed his fingers into her panties. "You this wet for me?" He groaned against her neck. "Jesus, Kimber."

He fingerfucked her as their mouths dueled for ownership. When her walls clamped down on his digits, Kimber cried out, flooding his hand with her juices.

"I need you inside me, Rory… now." She groaned as she continued to undulate her hips against him. He slipped his fingers free of her channel.

"You sure about this?" He searched her face for confirmation.

Bobbing her head as she tugged at his shirt, "Yes… I need to feel you."

Rory carried her over to the baby grand piano. "Will this hold you?"

She watched through hooded eyelids as he laid her on top of the smooth black surface. Tugging his belt free, he lowered his zipper and pushed down his pants enough to free his cock.

"Shit… Kimber, I don't have a condom. I wasn't planning on this when I came in here."

"I don't care… get over here and get inside me, Rory." She grabbed his hands and pulled him between her legs.

Rory tried to pull back, but she had other ideas and locked her feet behind his ass, jerking him forward. "Jesus, Kimber. *Wait.*"

"I'm on the shot… having a period while I'm—Never mind, it doesn't matter. Just fuck me already."

All the blood rushed to his dick as he pressed himself between her folds. No one, and he'd fucked plenty of women, ever felt like this. He wanted to pinch himself to make sure he wasn't dead because the way her pussy swallowed his shaft felt like heaven. When he bottomed out inside her womb, he leaned over her and captured her lips with his own. He pressed his tongue inside, tangling with hers. Her taste was addictive, and he knew without a doubt this wasn't going to be a one-time thing.

She lifted her hips, causing his hard member to pulse inside her channel. Taking the cue, Rory began to move, and fuck, if it didn't get even better. She made music like she was a star, but the way she took him inside her rivaled any harmony she could think of writing. They continued in a dance of sin, their moans and pants filling the music room with their own version of a symphony.

When he felt her body tighten beneath him, Rory reached between them and pinched the tiny pearl above her slit. Like a trigger, it sent her over the edge like a bomb detonating. Her walls locked down on his cock, almost to the point of being painful, and his body responded in kind. His orgasm ripped from him, and he spilled inside her. Never had he cum so hard in his life. Practically collapsing over her, Rory braced himself with his palms and lifted his spent frame to look her in the eyes.

"Damn… that was—" He shook his head, trying to find the words to explain what they'd shared. But the moment reality hit, he winced at the realization of what it meant.

"*Fuck*. Your brother is going to kill me."

CHAPTER FIVE

"WHY DO you look like someone killed your cat?" Atlas Lyons tossed a pen across the massive table they were all gathered around.

By 'they,' Rory meant his bosses, Atlas and Ares Lyons, plus Creed Sirius and Killian Jagger, the only other two members of the US-based division of Lyons Tactical. Atlas joined his older brother Ares Lyons when he left his career as a Navy SEAL and started Lyons Tactical Investigations. The baby of the family, Apollo, would officially join when his last enlistment was up. He was on leave at the moment and doing some recruitment for the company.

The company started out with international contracts, which consisted of just one team, currently deployed on an active case. Ares oversaw them from here and occasionally deployed with them. He limited his time away, so he ensured he could be here for his five-year-old son.

Ares started the company after his wife died while he'd been deployed on a top-secret mission. Unfortunately, he'd been targeted by the terrorists he was tasked with bringing down while overseas. Somehow, their target got word of the mission and sent some of his men to the US to send a message. His wife had been an easy target—completely unaware of the danger. Thankfully, his son was at daycare when she was murdered.

Rory glanced over at Atlas and smiled. "I don't have a cat, fucker."

"Must be over a girl, then. Babysitting getting on your nerves?" Killian glanced around at the men, smirking.

Rory sighed. The guys knew why he was staying at Jaxson's place—to watch over Jaxson's baby sister… only she wasn't a baby. Not by any stretch of the imagination. Kimber Storm was exactly the kind of woman who made his blood ignite into fiery desire. The way she fit around his cock was perfection. Then he went and fucked it all up. The moment the words slipped from his lips, a wall went up between them. She scurried out from under him and bolted from the music room, leaving him with his pants down around his thighs. He quickly tugged them up and went in search of her, only to find she had locked the door to the master bedroom and refused to open up and hear him out.

"Ah…" Rory palmed his neck. "I may have done something that pissed her off, and she isn't talking to me right now."

Creed barked out a laugh. "What the hell could you possibly have done to the woman? It's not like you're hooking up, so what's she got to be pissed about?" Atlas must've seen the way Rory winced because he snorted, "Shit, you *are* fucking her, aren't you?"

"It's not like that." Rory shook his head. "We hooked up once… and I might have mentioned that her brother was going to kill me." He sighed, frustrated with the radio silence she was giving him. "I promised him I'd look after her, not screw her."

"And that pissed her off?" Killian leaned back in his chair, his brows knitted in confusion. "I mean, you're not wrong. I don't have a sister, but if I asked a buddy to watch after my daughter, then they slept with her, I'd neuter them. So, yeah, Jaxson might actually pop one in you."

"I'm not sure if it's what I said… or when I said it."

Atlas tapped the surface of the table. "Please, for the love of all things holy, don't tell me you brought her brother up during sex."

"I don't know why I blurted it out…" Dropping his chin to his chest, Rory pinched the bridge of his nose. "It's just… ah… why does she have to be my best friend's sister?"

"Not to mention when she finds out you're living there because he wanted a babysitter for her, you're pretty well fucked." Atlas blew out a breath. "As interesting as this is, we have other matters to discuss. Ares wants me to hire some more people. I have a guy coming in from Atlanta, Luca Cashen. Former Army Medic worked for the Atlanta Fire Department and is moving to the area."

"Why the fuck would anyone move here? No offense, Atlas, but if you hadn't reached out to me, I wouldn't have picked this place on my own." Creed shifted in his chair and waited.

"Actually, he and I were medics together," Apollo spoke. "He heard about what we're doing and reached out. He'll be here tomorrow. We've split everyone into four teams. Team Atlas, headed by Atlas, obviously; Team Apollo, overseen by yours truly; Team Ares, which will be the international team already in place; and Team Hades will be the second international team."

"Team Hades?" Rory glanced around. "The others I get, but Hades? Who's gonna lead that one?"

"Me." Killian smiled. "Hades was my call sign in the SEALS."

"Each team will be composed of five members," Apollo continued. "One is the team leader; the others are men we've hired for their various skill sets. Sometimes, you'll work together, sometimes individually. Just depends on the needs of the clients. And there will be times when the US-based teams and international ones combine. When we started this, we weren't expecting it to grow so fast. Hell, it was just Killian, me, Ares, and Atlas. Then we brought on a few guys who'd transitioned to civilian life, and word got out. Luca will be one of many we hope to snag. Jaxson's already signed on; he's just wrapping up his commitment to the Navy. He'll be stateside in a few weeks."

"What about when we're not handling a detail? What do you want us to do?"

"Train."

Rory smiled. Ares recently purchased thirty acres of land, giving them a total of forty acres of wilderness. The facility was three miles from the main highway, tucked between a dense forest of trees and a massive lake. If you trekked a few miles beyond the lake, you'd run into some small mountains. The property comprised the main building, which was two stories situated over a basement, a dorm building that had enough rooms for each employee to live on-site without sharing a room, and of course, there was a mess hall in the main building. The best part, as far as Rory was concerned, was the training center. While Ares had spared no expense on any part of the complex, he went all out on a state-of-the-art gym/training facility. It had an indoor gun range, a swimming pool, and a weight room that had every piece of equipment imaginable. Ares was a firm believer that his men needed to stay in tiptop shape.

"Gentlemen." Ares stepped into the room. "I'd like you to meet Luca Cashen and Davis Lincoln. Luca was recruited by Atlas, but this guy,"—he turned and waved in Davis—"just fell into our laps this morning."

"Davis specialized in cyberwarfare and intelligence." Atlas smiled like he won the lottery—and chances were, he had with Davis.

"What branch were you?" Killian stood and shook his hand.

"Marines."

"You seem young. Why'd you get out?" It was Apollo who'd spoken.

They watched in shock as Davis tugged his pant leg up, exposing the steel limb hidden beneath the material. He tapped the iron rod before letting the fabric go.

"I was part of FORECON… until I wasn't."

Apollo let out a loud whistle. "Force reconnaissance unit… impressive. Damn, brother, you're gonna fit in just fine." Apollo stood and thrust his hand out to Davis. "And I'm calling dibs."

"Dibs?" Davis glanced around at the men. "I don't understand."

Ares growled as he rolled his eyes at his brother. "We've recently divided everyone into teams. Apollo here is staking his claim on you for when he gets out. Until then, you're going to be based out of here—headquarters. If I have my way, you won't be deploying and will oversee the cyber division once we add more people."

Rory listened as Apollo broke down the groups to Davis and Luca. He was so focused on listening to his boss that his cell phone nearly made him jump out of his seat. Sliding it out of his pocket, he furrowed his brow when he saw the contractor's number.

Call me asap...

"You alright?" Creed leaned over to him, glancing at Rory's cell phone.

"I don't know. I gotta message from the contractor." He stood and looked at the men gathered around the table. "Sorry, but I need to make a call."

Atlas started laughing. "Maybe don't talk about her brother this time."

Of course, he thought it was Kimber messaging him. Rory rolled his eyes as he pressed the contractor's icon. As the phone began to ring, he hung a bird at the men cackling behind him as he walked out of the room.

"Mr. Maverick, sorry to bother you," the older gentleman sighed. "Can you come home?"

"Did something happen?" He was already making his way out to his SUV. "I can head your way now."

Rory's heart pounded in his chest, a thousand scenarios playing through his mind. He'd finally decided he could leave her side for a few hours since she was at a local coffee shop with an old friend, and of course, something happened. How the hell was he going to look at his best friend now? Not only was he still trying to figure out how to tell Jaxson he'd slept with his sister, but now he was going to have to explain his house was damaged in an explosion.

"Mr. Maverick, did you hear me?"

Rory came back to himself and blinked. "What'd ya say, Hal?"

"I said there was a *small* explosion."

"Did you say explosion?" Despite trying his best to hold his shit together, Rory nearly ran off the road at her words. "*Shit.* I'm five minutes out."

Rory rounded the corner on two wheels and skidded to a stop in front of the house. He slammed the vehicle into park and bounded out of the car. He could see black smoke billowing up from the back of the house, making his heart jump inside his chest. As he was nearing the corner, he caught sight of the fire department dumping copious amounts of water toward the left corner of the home.

When his eyes landed on Hal, then on the backside of the house, he nearly pissed himself. Hal was holding a rag to his head, staring toward the back deck.

"What the fuck happened?"

Hal dropped the towel, exposing a small gash at his temple. He palmed the back of his neck and shrugged.

"Wish I could tell you that." He continued to hose down the smoldering planks of wood. "My guy was in the bedroom, and I was in the front of the house 'bout to head to my truck when the entire house rattled with an explosion. I stumbled to my knees—which is how I got this." He pointed to his head. "Coulda been worse had I still been in the kitchen."

"Anyone else hurt?" Rory scanned the yard, watching as the fire department extinguished the fire.

"Only the house." Hal shook his head. "I don't get it. We weren't messin' with anything that would have triggered this. Clark, my guy upstairs, said he thought the air conditioner made a weird clicking noise before the explosion happened, but he wasn't sure. Scared the shit outta him. I hate to tell you this, but her music room took some damage, too."

"Fuck." Rory was moving toward the house, his thoughts rolling over the what *if* Kimber had been here. He tamped down those thoughts and scanned the yard for someone in charge. He had to see for himself—that room was her sanctuary, and if it was ruined, he didn't know how she'd take it. "Excuse me." Rory stepped toward a man in turn-out gear standing near the front of the residence. "Am I able to go inside?"

The firefighter turned and narrowed his gaze on Rory. "And you are?"

Rory thrust his hand out. "Rory Maverick. I live here with Kimber Storm, one of the owners."

"Lieutenant Dawson." He held Rory's hand in a tight grip. "I just got word you can enter. My guys are still looking for the source, but they've turned off the gas to the house, so it's safe to check inside damage. I'll escort you since I need to see the inside myself."

As Rory followed him up the steps, he couldn't shake the feeling that maybe Jaxson was right—maybe there was more going on than Kimber let on.

CHAPTER
SIX

KIMBER SAT across from Sophie at Hounds and Grounds coffee shop, listening to her talk about her daughter, Chloe. It was hard to believe one of her closest friends growing up was a mother, and she'd had no clue. Guilt swirled inside her stomach as she scanned the images of the beautiful girl smiling back at her.

Kimber brushed her finger over the screen, "She's a cutie."

"Don't let that smile fool you. She's a terror on two legs." Sophie pulled her phone back and darkened the screen. "She's my universe, though. At some point, you'll get to meet Isaac. He's on a business trip right now."

"Tell me about him. Where did you meet?"

Sophie smiled, her face lighting up at Kimber's question. "Isaac and I met through a co-worker of mine. Stacey, the girl I work with, needed a wingman for a blind date she set up through

Bumble. I'd just started working at the elementary school and wanted to make friends. It was lonely after you and Avery left." Kimber started to apologize, but Sophie held her hand up. "Nope… you had your life, and I had mine. College kept me busy, Kimber, so I'm just as much at fault for losing touch. Besides, you're here now, and we can make up for lost time.

"Anyway," Sophie continued. "Isaac works in landscaping, a big company out of Birmingham. That's where he is right now. We dated for about six months, got pregnant, and eloped to Vegas. While my pregnancy might have spurred things along, we'd already been talking about marriage. His parents were not happy." Sophie sipped her drink.

"Because you got pregnant first?"

Shaking her head no, Sophie answered, "That probably didn't help, but they're this old southern family with lots of money. They had ideas for Isaac that didn't include marrying a small-town girl like me. Even though I got my degree from Auburn, they don't feel like I'm up to par for their only son. We hoped their granddaughter would mend the bridge they'd built between us, but it didn't. They see her twice a year—her birthday and Christmas."

"That's bullshit, Chloe." Kimber clenched her fist beneath the table. She hated stuck-up people, and hearing how Sophie's in-laws treated her stirred her disgust for that crowd. "What about your dad?" Sophie's mom died in a car accident when they were seniors in high school.

"He spoils her rotten. That's who has her now. Pops and Chloe are thick as thieves. Now that he's retired, he spends most of his time hanging out at the lake fishing or making my daughter more rotten."

A part of her couldn't help but be jealous of what Sophie had made for herself, as stupid as it was. Kimber had more money than she knew what to do with, yet she felt like something was missing.

"Tell me some more about Nashville. What's it like being around all those big stars?"

Kimber's lips twitched at the assumption she wasn't one of those *big* stars. Her identity as Stormer Hart and the Tempests had given her anonymity—and a heaping pile of loneliness. When Kimber had set out with Avery in tow, she never expected fame would equate to a small circle of friends. Her life comprised her manager, band mates, Avery, and Henley, her head of security. While Avery was the only friend from her past life, the others were just people who needed her. Kimber knew if push came to shove, they'd do what they needed to protect themselves. Stardom caused people to have loose attachments. How did she put what she was feeling into words without outing herself to her friend sitting across the table from her?

"Nashville is fast-paced and cutthroat. The music industry is hard and unforgiving, and I used to love it. Not so much anymore, which is why I'm home."

"I still can't believe you never got a serious record deal. You were always winning competitions at school. When Avery loaded your video onto YouTube, I thought for sure you'd struck gold."

"I do alright, but I needed a break." Kimber ignored the pain of her lies burning in her chest and forced a smile. "With Jaxson coming home in a few weeks, I wanted to be here to see him and help get the house in order."

"Why do I feel like you're leaving something out?" Sophie leaned back in her chair and smiled. "Kimber, we might have lost touch for the last decade, but friends like us don't lose that connection. What's going on? Did something happen in Nashville that sent you running back to Podunk, Alabama? Let's also not point out that you came home without Avery, your best friend who might as well be your sister. You two *went nowhere* without the other."

"Avery is a little preoccupied." Her mind conjured up Avery and Henley. The two of them were opposites, yet perfect for one another. "She's got a man now, and they're pretty serious. I am sure he's going to propose while I'm here."

"Wow… Avery is settling down. I never thought I'd see the day. She was loyal to you and wouldn't do anything that she thought would rock the boat. Any chance she'd come here for a visit? I'd love to see her."

"I'm sure I could get her here at some point."

"Sorry to intrude." The waitress stopped beside the table. "Can I grab you two something else to drink or eat?"

"Actually, I could use a refill, if you don't mind." Kimber watched as she poured the liquid gold into her cup and stepped away. "This place is pretty cool." She scanned the interior of the shop and noticed all the nuances. "They let dogs in here?"

"Yep, the owner is pretty cool. She comes over for ladies' night once a month. But stop avoiding my question, ma'am."

It was uncanny how, after all these years, Sophie could still read her like a book.

"I was just burned out and coming here lined up timing-wise. I miss my brother, and being here makes me feel connected to him."

Kimber smiled, thinking of her overbearing brother. Jaxson was off saving the world, and she was here feeling sorry for herself over a life that had left her wanting for nothing. Well, *almost* nothing. Her thoughts drifted back to the sexy man who'd given her the best orgasm of her life, only to ruin the moment by bringing up her brother.

"What caused that look?" Sophie arched a brow at Kimber.

"Nothing…" She sighed. "Okay, that's a lie." Kimber had kept enough from her friend, and since this was the one thing she could talk about, she decided Sophie was the perfect person to unload on. "Jaxson's best friend is staying at the house with me.

His place is being built, and since Jaxson's was sitting empty, he offered Rory a place to stay. Rory is going to oversee the contractor and his men."

"Okay… what aren't you telling me?"

Kimber tapped her fingernails across the surface of the table and bit down on her lip. "Well… he's been here ten days, and well, let's just say the rubber band I like to call 'sexual tension' snapped."

Sophie's eyes widened. "You're telling me you banged your brother's best friend?" Kimber nodded. "Was it at least good?"

"The best orgasm I've ever had," Kimber replied immediately. "Until he mentioned my brother, I was riding the post-orgasm endorphins."

"He didn't," Sophie giggled. "What a lady boner killer."

"Exactly. I simply slipped off the piano and hurried to my room." Kimber involuntarily shivered as the memory of his touch washed over her. Everything about Rory was sexy as hell… even his loyalty to her brother. That didn't stop her from being pissed off that he'd brought Jaxson up while he was still buried inside her.

Sophie's snort broke through the air, a mixture of amusement and envy coloring her tone.

"Wait, a minute… he fucked you on your piano? That's incredibly hot, Kimber. I've got to admit, I'm a bit jealous."

Kimber offered a nonchalant shrug, her expression a blend of reminiscence and wistfulness.

"It was really hot. I've never been intimate with anyone in my music room before, so it was definitely a first… and likely a last." She sighed, a tinge of regret seeping into her voice. "I've been steering clear of him ever since. I understand his loyalty lies with my brother, and knowing Jaxson, he'll have a fit. I'm not a child anymore, and God, Rory is exactly the kind of man I could easily fall for, but there's just too much standing in the way, too many obstacles between my bed and his."

"Let me guess," Sophie, ever observant, glanced slyly past Kimber and flashed a knowing grin. "Is Rory built like one of those guys you fantasize about in a steamy romance novel?"

Kimber's response was immediate, her voice tinged with longing. "Yep." She popped the 'p' emphatically, exhaling a deep breath. At that moment, her thoughts drifted to Rory, to the intensity of their connection and the undeniable physical attraction she felt for him. It was a desire tempered by the complications of their situation, a tantalizing 'what if' that lingered in her mind like the lingering notes of a haunting melody.

"And is he, oh… I don't know, six foot three or so with muscles you want to lick… and deep brown hair with dark eyes that scream danger?"

Kimber snorted as she picked up her coffee cup. "I don't know if I should be completely freaked out that you just described him to a 't' or if I should be reading some of your books to get my fill of the man I can't have."

"Oh, I'd say you're wrong on that account, Kimber…" Sophie's words were teasing, yet they carried an undercurrent of truth that resonated with Kimber. "Because if the look on that man's face says anything, it says he wants to bend you over this table."

Kimber's reaction was instantaneous. Her head snapped toward the door, her breath catching in her throat as she laid eyes on Rory. He was standing just a few feet behind her, exuding an intense, almost palpable aura. Despite the strikingly attractive man beside him, Kimber's gaze was fixated solely on Rory. His expression was one of raw desire, a look that seemed to echo Sophie's bold assertion with uncanny accuracy.

"Holy shit," Kimber whispered, a mixture of shock and a thrill coursing through her.

"Told ya," Sophie snickered, her eyes briefly darting to the handsome man at Rory's side. "Um… his friend is *hot*."

"Sophie," Kimber hissed, her heart pounding as Rory advanced toward her with a predatory grace. Every step he took was deliberate, heightening the electric tension between them. It was as if he were a lion, methodically closing in on his chosen prey, and she was his prey.

Sophie, unabashed and ever-playful, shrugged with a mischievous grin. "What? I'm married, not dead." Her comment cut through the thickening tension as Rory and his friend halted at their table.

"Kimber." Rory stopped beside her and nodded toward Sophie. "Ma'am, sorry to intrude, but I needed to speak with Kimber."

"Rory… this is my best friend from high school, Sophie. Sophie, this brooding man is Rory… *Jaxson's* friend." She hadn't meant for his name to come out so catty. "I'm Kimber." She stuck her hand out to the equally brooding man standing beside Rory. "And you are?"

"Atlas Lyons." His massive hand engulfed hers, and Kimber could swear she heard Rory growl.

Kimber's hackles went up, and she stiffened in her seat. If she remembered correctly, this was Rory's boss—and Jaxson's friend.

"Has something happened to Jaxson?"

"No… Shit, I didn't mean to give you that impression." Rory ran his fingers through his hair. "Jaxson's fine, as far as I know."

"Kimber," Sophie's voice cut through the panic rising inside her chest. "I'm going to go call my dad to come get me and let you work this out. Call me later so we can talk about ladies' night and piano lessons."

Kimber's gaze snapped to her friend, her cheeks warming with embarrassment. Sophie wasn't talking about music lessons at all, and from the surprised look on Rory's face, he knew exactly what her friend was hitting at.

"I'll take you home, ma'am." Atlas smiled at Sophie.

"Um… okay. Thanks." Kimber watched as Atlas helped Sophie to her feet.

"Rory, call me later and let me know if you need anything." Atlas slapped Rory on the back and waited for Sophie to say goodbye to Kimber.

She pushed to stand and tugged her friend into a hug. "I might kill you for that," she whispered into Sophie's ear.

"No, you won't. With the way that man is looking at you, he wants to devour you. Call me later, sweet cheeks. I missed you."

"Missed you, too." She watched as her friend strutted across the bakery with a sexy man at her side. She knew Sophie loved her husband, but what woman wouldn't eat up the attention the man was causing? He was hot as sin.

Taking a deep breath, she turned to face Rory. She let her gaze travel over his body before landing on his face. She expected to see anger there. Instead, red-hot molten desire burned in his eyes, making them black as coal. The way he was looking at her beneath hooded eyelids gave her the same rush she got performing… only her lady parts were pulsing with desperate need.

"Piano lessons, huh?"

CHAPTER
SEVEN

HE CALLED Atlas the minute he stepped out onto the porch of Kimber's house. The captain on scene said it looked like the gas line had ruptured, but until they could get an investigator out there from Birmingham, he wouldn't know for sure. Until then, he suggested they stay in a hotel. Atlas was concerned there was more going on, and promised to make a phone call to expedite the investigator. Having the Lyon brothers as bosses was proving to be a godsend. Rory was relieved when Atlas pulled into the driveway and stepped out of his SUV. He wanted to come and look at the damage himself.

"How bad was her music room?" Atlas kicked some of the charred debris out of the way. The wood was still warm in places and the scent of burning wood still filled the air. "Anything salvageable?"

"Her piano is toast." Rory grimaced. All he could see was her naked body leaning back on the keyboard as he licked her sweet spot before burying himself between her folds. "Her guitar was in a plastic case and beside the door. I grabbed it for her. This is going to be hard on her. From what Jaxson told me, the piano belonged to her aunt, the one who raised them. She's one of the reasons Kimber is trying to make it big."

Atlas mumbled something that Rory couldn't hear. "Well, I'll get Hilda to square away a place to stay for you guys. You sure you don't want to just use one of the dorm rooms?"

"No way. She still thinks I have a place being built. She'd probably wonder why I'm not staying on-site to begin with."

"You gonna call Jaxson?"

Rory scrubbed his hand down his face. "After I tell her."

Atlas nodded and headed toward his car. "I'll follow you there."

Atlas met Rory at the entrance.

"You come here before?" Rory watched as Atlas tugged the door open and ushered him through.

"Yeah, I bring Loki here once a week. He likes the back porch because he can wander around while I drink my coffee." Rory stopped dead, causing Atlas to walk onto his back. "Damn, brother, you've got it bad." He chuckled. "Hope she's worth the crushed ball sack when Jaxson hears about you fucking his sister."

"*Don't,*" Rory growled. "You might be my boss, but I will throat punch you if you talk about her like she's some chick I just picked up, Atlas."

"Oh, yeah…" Atlas clapped him on the shoulder. "This is going to be fun to watch."

Rory shrugged off his boss's hand and stalked toward Kimber. As he approached the table, his steps faltered when he heard her conversation.

"*I don't know if I should be completely freaked out that you just described him to a 't' or if I should be reading some of your books to get my fill of the man I can't have.*"

Her friend's eyes widened, but he could see the glint of humor in them. He waited to see if she outed him for overhearing, and when she didn't, he gave himself a mental fist pump. Rory planned to exploit the '*man I can't have*' part later on. For now, he needed to tell her about the house and their temporary home at the local motel. He worried she was going to be pissed about sharing a room—but hearing her conversation with her friend, he knew he'd get the chance to right his fuck-up.

Rory stifled a chuckle when her friend mentioned something about him bending her over the table and commenting that Atlas was hot. His boss blushed but pretended not to hear.

"Kimber." Rory pushed down the sudden blast of desire and nodded toward Sophie. "Ma'am, sorry to intrude, but I needed to speak with Kimber."

"Rory, this is my best friend from high school, Sophie. Sophie, this brooding man is Rory… *Jaxson's* friend." Kimber's tone was clipped, reminding him that he had some major groveling to do. "I'm Kimber." She stuck her hand out to the equally brooding man standing beside Rory. "And you are?"

"Atlas Lyons." Atlas smirked at Rory as he took Kimber's hand in his. Rory couldn't stop the growl from rumbling in his chest.

"Has something happened to Jaxson?"

Rory realized his mistake. She knew of Atlas and probably thought he was there with him to deliver bad news, even though the Navy would be the ones to make that kind of notification, not them.

"No… Shit, I didn't mean to give you that impression." Rory ran his fingers through his hair and sighed. "Jaxson's fine, as far as I know." He held her gaze.

He couldn't take his eyes off her and was desperate to know what she had said to Sophie about them. He chuckled to himself —*them*. There was not them, at least not yet. He couldn't deny his attraction to her, but if he was going to pursue her, he needed to talk to Jaxson.

"Kimber," her friend interrupted their stare off. "I'm going to go call my dad to come get me and let you work this out. Call me later so we can talk about ladies' night and piano lessons."

Rory didn't miss the comment—his eyes widened in surprise, but deep down, he was strutting around like a peacock. He was damn well certain Sophie wasn't talking about actual piano lessons. And that notion shot straight to his dick.

"I'll take you home, ma'am." Atlas's deep voice broke the lust haze he was in.

Rory smirked at Kimber when she glanced between her friend and Atlas.

"Um… okay. Thanks." Sophie took Atlas's hand and stood.

"Rory, call me later and let me know if you need anything." Atlas gripped his shoulder and squeezed.

Tipping his head, Rory watched as Atlas guided Sophie out the door. Turning his head back toward Kimber, he smiled.

"Piano lessons, huh?"

"Fuck…" Kimber's cheeks reddened, and she covered her face. "I hoped you hadn't heard that. And something tells me I couldn't convince you she really means piano lessons, can I?" She peeked up at him through her fingers.

"Not a chance in hell." He slid into the booth across from her. "And as much as I want to talk about her comment, I need to tell you something."

Kimber dropped her hands from her face and furrowed her brows. "This sounds serious?"

Rory inhaled and blew out his breath. He knew she was going to lose it, and he was debating on whether to wait and tell her in the car. Kimber being Kimber, she didn't let up.

"Well, spit it out. You're kind of freaking me out."

"Hal called me. There was a small explosion at the house." Kimber started to speak, but Rory held up his hand. "Before you ask, no one was hurt. Most of the damage is in the kitchen, but the rear of the house has some water damage." He waited for his words to sink in.

"My music room," she whispered, tears welling up in her eyes. "Is it gone?"

"Kimber, I'm so sorry, baby. The only thing salvageable was your guitar." She pushed out of the booth and darted toward the bathrooms. Rory was out of his chair chasing after her. "Wait, Kimber." The bathroom door slammed in his face, and he heard her breakdown on the other side. "Fuck." He glanced down the vacant hallway, and when he was certain no one was watching them, he pushed inside the women's restroom. He shut the door behind him and scanned the three stalls, spotting her feet under the largest one.

"Kimber, sweetheart." Rory pressed his hand to the closed stall. "Come out here so we can talk about it, babe."

"No. Please, Rory. Just let me be."

Rory peeked through the crack in the door and sighed in relief when he realized the stall was locked with a simple hook-and-eye style lock. He tugged his knife out of his pocket and flicked it open. Sliding the blade through the crevice, he unlatched the hook. Once he secured the blade in his pants, Rory pushed open the door and squatted down in front of Kimber, who was seated on the floor.

"Look at me, Kimber." He tipped her chin up with his fist. "I know what that piano meant to you, and I promise if it can be repaired, we'll get it done. But for right now, I need you to let me take you out of here."

Kimber sniffed and lifted her gaze to meet his. Her teal-green eyes shone back at him, and the look of utter loss nearly gutted him on the spot. He stood and tugged her from her stoop, then scooped her into his arms. Carrying her bridal style, he navigated them out of the bathroom and through the coffee shop. They got several curious stares, but no one bothered them as he got her out of there. Kimber didn't seem to notice that Rory had loaded her into his SUV and buckled her seatbelt. Atlas had sent him a text when they were inside telling him that Hilda reserved them a room at Sunny's, the local motel.

He pulled the car into the parking lot of the motel just as his phone beeped. Slipping the cell phone from his pocket, he glanced at the screen and smiled—Atlas.

Hilda went with Apollo to the house. They packed some clothes for both of you and some toiletries. Also grabbed her guitar. Everything is waiting for you at Sunny's.

Rory fired off a response, thankful his team had his back.

Thanks. She's taking this hard. Hasn't spoken since I told her.

Rory glanced over at Kimber and noticed she was quiet because she'd fallen asleep. It was still afternoon, but he figured the shock of what happened had sapped her of her energy. Just as he pulled into Sunny's, Atlas responded.

Call if you need anything. Got some people looking into the explosion. It's not looking like an accident. Might want to ask your girl if there's something we need to know. Jaxson had a gut feeling. Maybe he wasn't far off.

Rory hurried out of the truck and into the office. Once he had their room key, he rounded the front. Tugging open the door, he reached across and unbuckled her seatbelt. As he slipped his hands beneath her legs and pulled her against his chest, Kimber stirred against him.

"It's alright, I got you." He pressed a kiss to her forehead and carried her to their room. Balancing her in his arms, he got the door open and carried her inside. He swore when he noticed the king-sized bed against the far wall. The *one* bed in the room. "Shit," he whispered into the space. Moving to the edge, he laid Kimber down and pulled out his phone.

"You get into the room, okay?" Atlas's voice filled the line.

Rory pinched his nose. "What the fuck, Atlas? You put us in one bed. *One* bed."

"Yep. Best way to keep her safe. I'll call you if I get any updates." Atlas disconnected, leaving Rory to stare at his blackened screen.

His boss was fucking with him… had to be. There was no way he could share a bed with Kimber and not touch her. He glanced back at her sleeping form and groaned. Spying the bags near the door, Rory hurried over to them and squatted down. One of the duffels held all his weapons, the other had his clothes. Her suitcase was propped against the wall beside his stuff. Glancing at the clock, he sighed. It was only three-thirty in the afternoon.

"Rory." Kimber's sad voice forced him to turn around. She was watching him from the bed. "Can you lay with me? I know that's weird, but I just feel broken right now."

Fuck. This woman was testing all his limits.

"Sure." Rory walked around to the opposite side of the bed and pulled back the covers. "Climb under. Might as well take a nap. It'll make you feel better."

She scooted beneath the covers and waited for him to climb in. Once he was on his back, Kimber pressed her body against his, snuggling up to his warmth.

"Thanks."

"It's going to be okay, Kimber." Rory pressed a kiss to her head. "Close your eyes and rest. I've got you."

CHAPTER
EIGHT

THE VIBRATION of a phone on the nightstand roused Kimber. Stretching her body, her leg rubbed against a massive bulge covered in denim, and she froze. Her body was pressed flush against a firm body, one she'd felt before. Kimber blinked, clearing the confusion from her eyes.

"Stop thinking so hard," Rory's deep voice rumbled in his chest.

A chest she was lying across like she had done a thousand times, though she hadn't.

"What am I doing in bed with you?"

Rory chuckled beneath her, the sound sending pulses of need through her veins.

"What do you remember about earlier?"

That morning's events hit her like a bad movie on replay. She'd been having a good day with Sophie, catching up on old times, when Rory delivered the worst possible news ever. Not only had her aunt's house been damaged, the one connection Kimber cherished more than anything was ruined. God, she wanted to cry—again.

"Nah uh, princess. No more crying. I know my news wasn't what you expected, but we'll get everything fixed, I promise."

"You can't make that kind of promise, Rory." Kimber shifted, so she was leaning on his chest, looking into his face. "I need to see it. Can you take me over there?"

Rory brushed her hair from her face and smiled. "I'll make you a deal." He scooted back against the headboard and tugged her to sit up. "I'll take you there *if* after we can go out and have some fun."

"Fun? Rory, my brother's house was almost blown up. How can you possibly be thinking of fun right now?" Kimber slid off the bed and began to pace.

Rory joined her on the floor and watched her move back and forth. She probably looked like a cat on a hot tin roof, but in reality, Kimber wanted to scream. Was her past following her to Alabama, or was it really just an accident? Hell, the house was old, and the pipes might have been corroded as far as she knew. It's part of the reason she struggled with Jaxson's desire to keep it. *Shit*. Her brother. Kimber spun, nearly knocking into Rory, who was standing way closer than she realized. She pressed her hands into his chest before snatching them back as if she'd been burned.

"Does Jaxson know?"

Rory shook his head. "I was going to call him earlier, but…" He motioned to the bed.

"Call him. Please." Kimber placed her hands on her hips. "I don't want him to learn about this some other way. He'll worry about me."

Rory dipped his chin and moved to his duffle on the floor. He pulled out something that resembled a walkie-talkie, only larger. Keying in a few numbers, he pressed the device to his ear. It amazed her how easily he was able to get her brother on the phone when she usually had to leave a message and pray he'd call back within a few days.

"Ice… we got a situation. Can you talk?" Rory moved toward Kimber and rubbed her shoulder as he listened to whatever her brother was saying on the other side. Whatever it was, it must have been unpleasant, because Rory reached up and pinched the bridge of his nose. "Holy hell, brother, calm down. Kimber is fine. She's right here." Rory held the phone out. "You'd better talk to him. He won't let me get a word in edge-wise."

Kimber rolled her eyes and fisted the phone. Pressing it to her face, she sighed.

"Hello, big brother."

"What the fuck, Kimber? I've only got one more month, and my best friend calls to say you have a situation. Start talking."

Jaxson's voice was all growly, as it had been for most of her teenage years. His overprotectiveness was the reason she could never get a boy to date her—between his threats and overbearing attitude, no guy was daring enough to pursue her.

"Oh, calm down, you alphahole. I'm fine. Your house, on the other hand, is not. I'm so sorry, Jax. I don't know what happened."

"Wait… this isn't about whatever had you running like your ass was on fire away from Nashville?"

Kimber jerked. "What? I wasn't run—"

"Don't, Kimber," he cut her off. "I know you're hiding something—what, I'm not sure. But cut this shit, baby sister of mine. We can skip that conversation for now, but I'm going to figure out what you're hiding. What happened to the house?"

Kimber pinched her nose and explained what little she knew. Jaxson assured her a house was replaceable. She was not. He encouraged her to change the kitchen, since it was demolished, anyway. Somehow, she found the strength to tell him about the piano without crying.

When her Aunt Maggie took them in as kids, she forced Kimber to focus her anger on music—refusing to let her give it up. It was hard to do something that had been her and her mom's thing, but the keys of the piano felt right under her fingers. The piano was hers. When she mentioned the piano, Jaxson grew quiet on the other end. Kimber knew he was feeling her pain through the phone. They were close like that.

"Aw, shit, Kim. I'm sorry about that. Maybe it can be fixed. Hey, look, put Rory on the phone and do me a favor. Go out tonight and forget all about the house for a bit. I'll get with him on what to do now. Don't worry about it, sis, and the other stuff. We will talk about it later. I haven't forgotten you're not telling me everything."

"Fine, whatever. Here, he wants to talk to you. That my stuff?" Kimber pointed to the suitcase near a green duffle bag. Rory nodded and continued talking to her brother. "Great, I'm going to shower."

Kimber opened the bag and retrieved some jeans, underwear, and a shirt. She shot Rory one last glance, then headed into the adjoining bathroom. Leaning against the countertop after she set her clothing on the edge, she stared at her reflection. She looked like someone had poured salt in her eyes. They felt gritty from all the crying she'd done. Her life was going to *shit*. She'd been in Alabama for a little over a month and still had no answers about what to do with her career. Maybe having a stalker was good for her—it forced her home to reevaluate her life. Or lack thereof. Sure, she had music and her band, but what else?

Pushing off the porcelain, she turned on the water and began stripping off her clothes. Kimber was about to step into the tub when a knock at the door stopped her. Grabbing the towel, she wrapped it around her body and prepared herself to face the man at the door. A man, for all purposes, who was off-limits. A man she should be furious with but wanted, despite him ruining the best sex she had by bringing her brother into the moment. Closing her eyes, she fisted the knob and called out.

"Yeah?"

"You okay?" Rory's voice filtered through as Kimber cracked open the door and peeked out.

"I'm fine."

Rory's eyes scanned her bare shoulders and growled. Kimber could see the pulse throbbing in his neck. His fingers gripped the wooden edge as his eyes burned with need.

"Tell me to go, Kimber." His voice rumbled as he watched, waiting for the sign she didn't want what they both needed.

Kimber needed to do something normal—something that let her forget about her stalker... the explosion. Not thinking of the ramifications, Kimber pushed open the door, stepped back, and dropped the towel. Rory's eyes dilated as he pushed through the open space, cupped her cheeks, and backed her against the countertop. His mouth descended like a heat-seeking missile, and once he covered hers, it was an explosion of built-up tension they'd been holding onto. Kimber tore at his shirt, demanding it off with her hands. She needed to feel his skin on hers.

Rory let go of his hold on her face long enough to break their kiss and give her the space needed to remove the fabric. Once she had his chest bare, her fingers danced along the plains of his defined abs, tracing their way down. Her hands attacked his jeans, pulling the belt undone and tossing it to the floor. He kissed her lips, licking at the seam, demanding entry.

As their tongues dueled, Kimber got his button open and pushed her hand beneath the material covering the steel shaft she remembered moving inside her only days ago. As her fingers wrapped around his rock-hard cock, Rory let out a growl against her lips. Stepping back, he shoved his pants down and kicked them off with his shoes. He grabbed Kimber and lifted her, so she had no choice but to wrap her legs around his waist. In two steps, he had her inside the shower, hot water cascading around them.

Every touch, every nibble, sent a fire of desire through her body.

"Please… I need you inside me."

Rory pressed her back against the fiberglass wall and held her tight with one arm as he guided his aching member between her legs. Kimber moaned as he filled her, her nails scoring her mark across his back. They found a rhythm beneath the spray—two bodies in tune with one another. Kimber felt the sensations start at her toes and climb their way to her center. When her body tightened, Rory pushed faster, his own climax demanding to be part of the moment.

When their breaths finally slowed, Rory leaned back and held her gaze. Slowly dropping her to her feet, he spun her around and kissed her shoulder. He grabbed the tiny bottle of body wash and squirted it in his hands. His palms glided over her skin, lathering up the parts he had yet to touch. When he had covered her entire body in suds, he rinsed her skin clean. Turning her to face him, he held her gaze and opened his mouth to speak.

"I—"

Kimber placed her finger over his lips, silencing his words.

"Don't mention my brother. Not while you're naked in the shower with me. You did that once when we were together. Let's not make it twice."

Rory barked out a laugh. "I wasn't going to mention your *brother,* beautiful. I was going to say I can't stay away from you. Nor do I want to. Now…" He cut the water off and helped her out of the enclosure. Rory grabbed a fluffy white towel, wrapped it around her, and leaned in for a gentle kiss. "Let's get dressed, have some dinner, and come back here so I can truly worship your body like it deserves."

"Okay."

Kimber followed him into the bedroom, clutching the clothes she'd brought into the bathroom. She watched unashamedly as he bent down and dug through his own duffle. He glanced over his shoulder and smirked.

"Like what you see?"

"Um… yeah." Kimber snorted. "I do." She bit her lip and gave him a dose of his own medicine. She turned and bent down to ease her panties over her feet. Giving a quick glance over her shoulder, she saw Rory standing by his bag. He hadn't put on a shirt, and his jeans were unbuttoned and open. She gasped when she realized he was fisting his cock.

Shimmying the silky thong up her legs, she slipped the material over her backside. When she chanced another look, she was startled by Rory's body tackling her from behind and lifting her off the floor. He dove with her in his arms onto the bed and rolled her over, so she was under him.

"We were supposed to go to dinner." Rory brushed her still-wet hair from her face.

She shrugged. "I'm not super hungry. Maybe I still need to work up an appetite."

CHAPTER
NINE

KIMBER APPEARED stunning in jeans and a cotton t-shirt, with her cowboy boots accentuating the allure of her legs. Despite her outward beauty, a trace of sadness marred her features as she gazed at the house for the first time since the explosion. Standing beside Kimber, it was evident the feelings of pure happiness they had experienced just an hour ago had dissipated, replaced by a somber atmosphere as they stared at the back of her house. Rory felt the impulse to reach out and comfort her, but he knew it wasn't the right time, especially with Hal standing beside her. Kimber's gaze remained fixed on the burned-out remnants of the back deck, the lingering scent of charred wood still permeating the air.

"Well… standing here isn't going to change a damn thing. Is it safe to go inside?" Kimber looked over at Hal. "I'd like to see the rest of the destruction."

Hal gave her a slight nod. "I can show you."

"No." Kimber closed her eyes and inched forward toward the house. "Sorry. I'd like to see it alone."

"I-I don't know how safe the floor is in certain areas, Miss Storm," Hal stammered, his uncertainty of letting her go inside alone clear in his tone.

"I'll take her." Rory stepped forward and gripped Kimber's elbow in his hand. "She'll be safe with me."

Rory led Kimber up the stairs, what was left of them, and navigated them into the remains of the kitchen. He didn't know what to say to make the situation any easier. Rory suspected she didn't really care about the kitchen, knowing it was going to be redone, anyway. That's not what had her in tears only hours before. Her heart had been breaking for losing her piano, the one thing she'd shared with her aunt.

Following behind her to ensure she didn't step on any weakened floorboards, Rory pressed behind her as she stopped in front of the closed door to her music room. If there had been no damage visible damage anywhere else, one wouldn't know there had been an issue standing outside the door. But Rory knew better—he'd seen what was in store for her beyond the barrier.

"You ready?" He pressed his hand to her shoulder.

Kimber took a deep breath and sighed, "Not really, but I need to see it for myself."

Reaching around her body, Rory turned the knob, shoved the door open, and eased Kimber's body forward. She stumbled when her eyes landed on the destruction inside. Had he not been standing behind her, Rory was convinced she would've fallen. The intake of breath cut at his insides, but Kimber didn't speak. Instead, she carefully walked around the space, stopping directly in front of the piano.

"I learned to write music on this. Did I tell you that?" Rory didn't speak. He knew she wasn't really talking to him. "My aunt wanted me to have an outlet for my grief. Losing my parents was hard, but I picked up the pieces and moved on. For them. I had to. She sat with me for hours the week following their funeral. We sat on the bench and played until our fingers bled. Losing this is like losing them all over again." Kimber turned, her eyes glistened with tears. "I don't want to cry anymore, Rory. I hate this."

He stepped forward and wrapped her in his arms. Rory pressed his lips to her head and whispered against her hair, "I'll do everything I can to get it fixed. If it's possible, Kimber, I promise you I'll make it happen. Now,"—he leaned her away from his muscular frame to look her in the eyes—"how about we go grab some food and have a little fun?"

She took a deep breath and nodded. "You know what... yeah. Let's go have some fun."

They carefully walked out of the room and through the house. Rory led her down the front steps and to his truck. After helping her inside, he rushed around the front and climbed inside.

"Do you trust me?"

Kimber glanced over at him, "Of course."

Rory smiled and threw the SUV in reverse. He tore down the driveway like a madman, eager to make her forget about the things in his rearview mirror. Kimber's laughter filled the Tahoe, making him smile. If his crazy driving was what it took to make her laugh, he'd gladly let her giggle at him. Kimber sat quietly, staring out at the landscape as they drove down the main street. Copper Springs was home to around twenty thousand people. It was small, but not so small you knew everyone's business. Rory felt way more at ease here than he had in Los Angeles, home of the rich and famous. When Ares reached out and offered him the job, he hadn't hesitated. He had grown to loathe famous people in the brief time he worked in Hollywood as a glorified babysitter. Being here, in small-town Alabama, Rory felt at peace. And having the beautiful woman sitting next to him made it even better.

The cab was eerily quiet except for the music playing. Rory reached across and turned up the volume when one of his favorite songs came on. He tapped out the beat on the steering wheel, thinking about how much he hated to love the song. The band Stormer Hart was your typical pop group—a group of women who'd sold their identities to a label for money. Rory snorted.

"What's so funny?" Kimber shot him a curious look.

Rory shook his head and grinned. "Nothing, just thinking about how much I hate this group, but really like the song."

Kimber blinked at his admission. Rory watched a weird expression filter across her face.

"You hate the band?"

He nodded, "Yeah. I do."

Kimber stiffened in her seat. "Why, it's not like you know them personally."

Rory cleared his throat. "You're right, I don't know *them*, but I do know musicians just like them. They sold themselves to become what society said they should be. Controlled by the label, and their lead singer probably can't even sing without auto-tune."

Kimber flinched at his words, as though what he'd said was about her. He started to ask why his opinion of the iconic band mattered, but she spoke before he could.

"Where are we going?"

"Well, I thought we could both use a drink and maybe some *real* music. So, we're going to Off Duty."

Off Duty was a bar owned by a former Marine and his retired police officer wife. They wanted to create a space where anyone felt safe to relax and enjoy themselves after a hard day. Of course, their primary clientele was public servants, but many of the town's folk hung out at the bar, too. Guess they felt safe, seeing as they were almost always surrounded by off-duty cops and firemen.

Rory pushed down his unease over her reaction and forced a grin as he pulled the truck into the lot. It was pretty crowded, but he expected nothing less. It was karaoke night. While he dared get on stage, he enjoyed listening to others try their best to hold a tune. He figured Kimber might enjoy letting go and, who knows, maybe sing.

As they climbed out of the SUV, Rory was slightly worried he'd made a mistake. Kimber had said nothing about where they were, nor had she looked at him. It was as if her mind was stuck on what he'd said on the ride over.

"Kimber, wait up." He jogged to catch up as she pushed through the entrance.

The sound of someone belting out Janis Joplin's '*Bobby McGee*' blared throughout the bar. Kimber looked over her shoulder at Rory and grinned.

"Karaoke night, huh?"

"Yeah, I just thought maybe you'd have some fun. Maybe even sing."

"I bet they don't have *auto-tune* here." She smirked. "Good thing I can sing."

Rory followed her toward a table in the back. She commandeered the space and slid into the booth. He watched as she scanned the bar and sighed.

"You want to sing?"

His hands reached across the wood surface and tugged hers into them. She glanced down at their entwined hands and smiled. At least she wasn't pulling them away. That had to say something. Rory wasn't sure what he'd said that had offended her. Unless someone had accused her of using audio enhancement to sing, he wasn't sure what happened in the SUV.

"Hey, I'm sorry if what I said in the car upset you. I guess I'm just jaded from my time babysitting Hollywood."

"It's fine, Rory." She waved him off. "It's just… you were probably right. They are most definitely singing what they're told. It's that way in the business. If you want to make it big, you practically have to sell your soul."

"Is that what happened to you? Is that why you came home?"

She held his gaze as if searching for the words to respond. Rory held his breath. He needed her to open up to him and tell him whatever it was she was hiding. He believed Jaxson wasn't far off—her trip home was more than wanting to help her brother. She was hiding something, and he was determined to show her that she could trust him. Hell, he wanted her to give him her worries and let him in.

"I think I'm going to go pick a song. Order us some wings and beer." She shot him a sassy grin. "You were right… I needed this." He watched as she hurried over to the DJ and spoke to him.

"Hey, handsome." The waitress appeared at his side, her perfume nearly gagging him. "What can I get ya?"

Rory placed his order with the waitress, forcing a smile that didn't quite reach his eyes. "A dozen mild wings and a pitcher of Michelob Ultra, please." His tone was casual, but his mind was elsewhere, reflecting on the evening's events, which gave the illusion he was waiting for the waitress to do something.

The waitress, perhaps misreading the situation, leaned in a little too close for comfort. Her hand rested gently on his shoulder as she asked in a soft tone, "Anything else?"

Before Rory could respond, Kimber's voice sliced through the moment, sharp and unexpected. "Pretty sure he told you every-thing. So how about you take your hand off his arm and be on your way?" Her words were laced with a protective edge, a clear boundary being drawn.

The waitress seemed taken aback, her eyes darting rapidly between Rory and Kimber, as if trying to gauge the dynamics of the situation. "Um… sure. Sorry, sugar. I'll get this in right now," she stammered, her demeanor shifting from flirtatious to flustered in an instant.

Kimber watched the waitress abscond hastily, almost as if fleeing from an uncomfortable situation. Rory, unable to contain himself, burst into laughter. The tension of the moment dissolved into humor.

"Damn, woman. I think you scared the shit outta our waitress," he exclaimed, his laughter ringing out in the space between them.

Kimber, unapologetic yet slightly embarrassed, shrugged. "Sorry. I can't stand women like her. You're obviously with me, even if we aren't…" She gestured vaguely between them, struggling to find the right words. "You know."

"No, darling. I don't know," Rory teased, playing along, his voice laced with a hint of flirtation. He reached out, taking her hand gently and brushing his thumb across her knuckles. "What aren't we?"

Kimber let out a frustrated growl, her emotions tangled. "You know… a couple," she finally admitted, revealing the unspoken tension between them.

Before Rory could delve deeper into their conversation, Kimber's name was called out.

"Looks like I'm up," she announced, a hint of relief in her voice as she used the opportunity to escape the intensity of their exchange.

"We aren't done talking, Kimber," Rory called out after her, his eyes following her as she moved toward the stage, a playful smirk on her face. She gave him a small wave, a gesture that was both a goodbye and a promise of more conversations to come.

As Kimber gracefully made her way onto the stage, Rory's attention momentarily shifted when he noticed his boss, Atlas, approaching him. Rory acknowledged Atlas with a subtle nod, tipping his jaw in a silent greeting as Atlas took a seat across from him.

"How's your girl doing?"

Rory responded to Atlas's question with a light-hearted chuckle. "My girl?" he echoed, the term seeming almost foreign in the perspective of his and Kimber's complex relationship.

"Yep, dipshit. Your girl," Atlas retorted with a familiar, teasing bluntness that was characteristic of their relationship.

"About to sing, actually." He glanced toward the stage, his gaze softening. "Thought it would take her mind off things."

Atlas was about to comment, perhaps to tease Rory further or offer some insight, but his words were halted as Kimber's voice began to fill the room. The sound of her singing seemed to cast a spell over the entire space. The melody of Natalie Jane's *Intru-*

sive Thoughts' started to play, but it was Kimber's unique rendition that captivated everyone. Her voice, smoky and resonant, weaved through the lyrics with an emotional depth that you could almost touch.

The hair on Rory's arms stood at attention as he lost himself in the music. He felt as though Kimber was communicating with him through her performance, sending him a message that was both intimate and profound. The emotions the song stirred in him were intense, leaving him with a sense of longing he didn't understand. Rory couldn't help but feel that Kimber was revealing something personal, something meaningful, through her song.

"Damn, Rory. I think you're screwed, brother."

The crowd roared, demanding an encore. Kimber smiled and nodded toward the DJ. This time, the song that started nearly took the air out of his lungs. It wasn't a love song, per se. It was a message of hope, a plea for someone to save her. And God damn, Rory planned on doing just that. He was so lost in the words of Alexander Stewart's *'If you only knew,'* he didn't see Atlas get up. When Kimber hit the last note of the song, Rory was already across the floor. He reached up and plucked her off the stage, and pulled her body to his. His lips covered hers, making the patrons go even crazier with applause.

"Thanks." Kimber laughed against his lips. "I take it you liked the songs?"

"Liked?" Rory set her down, "No, Darling, I loved them."

Rory led her to the table where their food and beer were waiting. He pressed one more kiss to her lips before helping her slide into her seat. Sitting across from her, he just stared in wonder.

"Darling, you've got a hell of a gift, so I'm going to need you to tell me why you left Nashville instead of trying to get a recording deal."

"I was burned out." Kimber seemed to choose her words wisely. "I've been at it a long time, Rory. And well… I just needed a break."

CHAPTER
TEN

She sensed Rory's skepticism, and a part of her yearned to divulge the truth to him. However, confessing her real identity and the purpose behind her presence would set off a chain of events she wasn't ready for, at least not yet. Kimber relished the newfound freedom of being an ordinary person, a departure from the constraints of her celebrity status. Besides, during the ride to the bar, Rory had expressed a disdain for famous individuals. If he discovered her true identity, he might develop a strong aversion toward her, and the thought of him hating her was something she wasn't prepared to handle. Especially not when she found herself drawn to the brooding hunk.

Acknowledging the incompatibilities between them, Kimber recognized that Rory was, in many ways, wrong for her. The most significant obstacle was the fact that he was her brother's best friend. Jaxson was going to blow a gasket when he found out about them—that is, if she kept her *other* secret from him. Kimber couldn't afford to let Rory in on why she was really in Alabama, knowing that it might shatter the delicate balance she was desperately trying to maintain.

"I'll stop pushing for now." Rory brushed his fingers across her knuckles. "But eventually, you need to trust me." He chugged his beer and set the glass down.

"Did I see your boss earlier?"

Rory scanned the bar. "Yeah, he was here. Wonder where he…. What the hell?" Rory blinked, causing Kimber to crane her neck in the direction he stared. "That's not something you see every day."

At the bar, a woman clad in a wedding dress caught Kimber's attention. Despite still wearing her veil, she unapologetically downed a shot of amber liquid. "I can't fathom why a bride would be seated alone in a bar, indulging in drinks." Kimber voiced her concern, casting a worried glance at Rory. "Should we go over and check on her?" Rory was about to push to his feet when Kimber jerked his hand. "Hang on. Looks like Atlas is checking on her."

They watched as he saddled up to her at the bar and leaned in. Rory and Kimber were captivated by the scene as the woman turned toward him, breaking into laughter. She playfully spun her finger in the air before returning her focus to her drink. Atlas shot Rory a look that left Kimber puzzled, a blend of anger and a demeanor reminiscent of a scorned child. Suppressing a chuckle, Kimber instinctively covered her mouth. Regrettably, the music failed to mask the sound, and Rory turned in her direction.

"Giggling at my friend, Kimber?" his tone was filled with mirth. "Looks like he was tongue-lashed by the bride. And I don't mean the kind of tongue that leaves you feeling good." Rory's facial expression was dead serious as he muttered the words, causing Kimber to roar with laughter.

"Hope I'm not interrupting." A sweet-sounding voice broke the trance Kimber was stuck in. When she finally tore her gaze from Rory, she found her friend Sophie with a man standing beside their table.

Kimber glanced at Sophie, "Oh my God, Soph." She jumped out of her seat and wrapped her friend in a hug. "What the heck are you doing here?"

Sophie giggled and pulled back, her eyes shifting to the man at her side. "Kimber, this is my husband Isaac. Isaac, this is one of my oldest friends, Kimber."

Isaac held his hand out and gripped Kimber's hand in his. "Pleasure to meet you, ma'am."

Kimber grinned. "Oh wow. It's nice to meet you. Sophie, Isaac, this is my friend, Rory." She waved her hand at him, noting the slight growl at her description of him. Sophie's eyes widened as she covered her mouth to hide the chuckle.

"Nice to meet you." Rory shook Isaac's hand as well. "Would you like to join us?"

Kimber nodded as she shimmied into the seat beside Rory. "Yes, please, sit."

When Sophie described Isaac, the man occupying the booth across from her didn't quite fit the image she had painted with her words. The man before her appeared weathered, his features etched with the wear and tear of life's challenges. As Sophie continued to talk, Kimber's gaze unintentionally drifted to Isaac's tired eyes. Dark circles clung beneath them like shadows that had lingered for far too long.

"So, Isaac." Rory rested his palm against Kimber's leg and squeezed. "What is it you do for a living?"

Isaac shifted in the booth. "A little of this, a little of that."

"He's being shy. Isaac works for GreenYard out of Birmingham. He's their head arborist."

"Wow." Kimber took a sip of her drink. "That must be hard work."

"It is." Isaac was rather short in his words, making it seem he wanted to be anywhere but there.

Kimber cast a subtle glance at her friend, her eyes scanning the familiar contours of a face she had known for years. Despite the surface-level joy of their reunion, Kimber's intuition whispered that beneath the smiles, her friend was harboring a well-concealed sadness. Kimber resolved to tread carefully, sensing that beneath the layers of smiles and laughter, there was a secret her friend was unwilling to admit or share. Desperate to avoid asking her friend what was wrong, she turned to happier topics.

"Where's Chloe tonight?"

"Babysitter." Sophie shrugged. "Isaac and I haven't had much time alone, so we thought we'd come out tonight and enjoy adult time."

Isaac waved a waitress over and ordered a pitcher of beer. Kimber listened as Sophie talked about her week at work. The entire time, Isaac looked increasingly miserable. She was about to suggest they go dancing and leave the men to chat when Rory leaned over and whispered in her ear.

"I think your friend's husband wants to be anywhere but here."

She turned her face toward him and shrugged. "I think you're probably right."

"Maybe we should excuse ourselves, so we aren't crowding their time together. Besides, I could think of a few more entertaining things we can do alone."

Kimber blushed but nodded. "Sophie." She got her friend's attention. "I think Rory and I are gonna head out. Call me later this week, and we'll grab some coffee. Besides, I want to meet Chloe."

"Yeah," Sophie sighed. "I think we're going to head out, too. Isaac is over this place."

Kimber hated the way her friend's shoulders sagged. Maybe her marriage wasn't the picturesque haven Kimber had conjured in her imagination—a sanctuary of love and bliss. The reality, it seemed, wore a more somber hue. Kimber knew what loneliness looked like, and she was sure her friend was wearing the telltale coat Kimber had been wearing for a while now.

With a heavy heart, they slipped out of the booth, the muffled sounds of the restaurant creating a backdrop to the unspoken worries between friends. Kimber couldn't shake off the worry that clung to her like a persistent shadow. She inhaled sharply, a reflex to hide the depth of her concern, as they bid their farewells. The night, once filled with laughter and shared moments, now carried the weight of unspoken fears as Kimber grappled with the insight that her friend's perfect façade harbored cracks that mirrored the fractures in her own carefully constructed reality.

"You have a good heart, Kimber." Rory pulled her back to his front. "You're worried about your friend, I can tell."

She cocked her head to look up at him. "Yeah. She just looks so sad."

Rory followed her friend's retreat and sighed. "You never know what secrets someone is hiding." Kimber stiffened in his hold, her mind thinking about the secrets she was still hiding from him. "Maybe one day she'll open up to you. Until then, just be there for her. Secrets are nothing but poison and eventually pollute even the strongest relationships. If he's hiding something, she'll need you when the time comes."

Kimber climbed into Rory's SUV, the door closing behind her with a soft thud that seemed to resonate in the silence. As she sank into the plush seat, her fingers trembled slightly as they fumbled with the seatbelt, a tangible sign of the internal turmoil she couldn't escape. The metallic click echoed louder than she expected, a stark reminder of the choices she had made and the lies she was living.

Rory was everything she wanted but couldn't have. The mirage of a life she would never truly experience—especially not as Stormer of Stormer and the Hearts. Rory had been pretty clear when he'd mentioned despising musicians and movie stars. No matter how desperately she wished otherwise, Kimber couldn't shake the feeling that she was merely a fleeting chapter in Rory's life—a chapter destined for closure.

"Kimber," he whispered, the weight of concern clear in his voice. "There's something on your mind. I can feel it. Talk to me." Rory's gaze intensified, his curiosity mingling with concern. At that moment, the secrets she had been trying to hide threatened to spill out.

"Rory," Kimber began tentatively, her voice carrying the weight of the secrets she carried. She glanced at him, her eyes searching for a connection that could bridge the gap between her hidden truths and the vulnerability she wanted to share.

Rory's gaze was steady, a mixture of concern and genuine curiosity etched on his face.

"You can tell me anything, Kimber. I'm here for you."

Kimber felt a sudden surge of anxiety. The weight of the truth pressed upon her chest, and doubt crept into her mind like darkness. Suddenly, Kimber paused. The confession remained on the tip of her tongue, but something held her back. She looked away, breaking the connection with Rory.

"It's nothing. I'm just tired," she whispered, her voice barely audible above the car's hum.

Rory held her gaze momentarily before redirecting his attention to the road. In silence, he skillfully maneuvered the Expedition into the motel parking lot. Bringing the SUV to a halt, he turned off the engine and faced her. "Let's get you inside, Kimber."

She nodded in agreement and pushed open the door. Rory was right there as she descended to the ground, his firm grip on her elbow guiding her onto the walkway in front of their room. Affixed to the exterior was an envelope devoid of a postmark.

Rory swiftly removed the card from the surface and tore open the envelope. "Fuck."

"Wh-What does it say?" Kimber snatched the folded paper from his hand and read the ominous words scrawled on the parchment.

Does he know your secret? I do… but soon, it won't matter.

Kimber exhaled deeply, silently praying that Rory wouldn't meet her gaze as she posed a question to which she already knew the answer.

"Do you think someone taped it to the wrong door?"

With her hands thrust into her pockets, she battled against the tears that lurked perilously close to the surface. The last thing she wanted was to break down in front of him. Doing so would jeopardize her ability to keep her identity under wraps, and she wasn't prepared to reveal the truth just yet.

Rory shook his head. "I don't know. It's strange, though." He cast a sidelong glance at Kimber, and she could almost sense that he saw through her attempts at deception. Rory, not one to be fooled easily, likely had a sixth sense honed by his background, telling him that the note was meant for her. Kimber, however, maintained a nonchalant shrug, avoiding any indication that she shared his suspicion.

"Let's get inside. I'm going to call our computer guy and see if he can locate any cameras in the area. I doubt this place has any," Rory declared.

"Why would you do that? It's just some random note, Rory."

As Kimber moved toward the room, Rory extended his arm, halting her steps.

"Let me check it out first."

Grumbling about his overprotectiveness, Kimber waited patiently as Rory meticulously cleared the motel room. Once assured that no immediate dangers lurked, he signaled for her to follow. Despite her reluctance, Kimber couldn't shake off the unsettling thought that her potential stalker had found her. She stomped toward the bed and took a seat. The last thing she wanted was for him to spend any time potentially revealing why she was home.

"I don't see what the big deal is. Let's just go to bed. Please, Rory. I'm exhausted."

Rory stood there for a beat before finally nodding. "Fine, it can wait until tomorrow."

Kimber let out a sigh of relief. At that moment, all she desired was to nestle against his powerful frame and temporarily forget about her troubles. Rory had a way of making her feel ordinary, and she was determined not to let her past cast a shadow over the present. Without wasting a moment, she discarded her clothes and opted for one of Rory's t-shirts. Pulling it over her head, she settled into the bed, observing Rory as he secured the room. To her surprise, he revealed a gun from his boot, placing it on the nightstand beside the bed.

Rory methodically removed his boots and jeans, adding them to the pile with hers. He then tore his shirt off, leaving him in a pair of fitted boxer briefs. Slipping into bed beside her, he opened his arm, inviting her to snuggle closer. Kimber gladly nestled into his embrace and closed her eyes. In that moment, she allowed herself to imagine she was an ordinary woman, wrapped in the arms of a man she was swiftly falling in love with. The thought quickened her heartbeat. Rory wasn't someone she could have for the long term, and parting ways with him in a few weeks would likely be more painful than she expected. Nevertheless, she was going to enjoy the risk of falling in love—even if it meant her heart might break later when she had to walk away.

CHAPTER
ELEVEN

RORY EXPRESSED gratitude for Hal's swift repairs to the kitchen, allowing them to move back into the house. The motel had become an unwelcome place, especially after the unsettling note taped to the door. Kimber's reaction spoke volumes, confirming to him that she was concealing something, aligning with her brother Jaxson's suspicions. Now, seated at the table with his boss and the new computer expert, Davis, Rory felt a rising frustration.

"The traffic camera across the street from the motel room captures someone in a hoodie approaching the door about twenty minutes before you two arrive. Based on the build, I'm inclined to believe it's a man, but he deliberately avoids showing his face. It seems he was aware of the nearby camera," Davis reported.

"Fuck." Rory tousled his hair with his fingers. "So, she's keeping something under wraps. According to the note, someone is aware of it and essentially threatening to reveal her secret." He glanced at Atlas, noting his boss seemed to shift nervously in his seat. "What? Do you know something?"

"Listen, Rory. You and she need to have a conversation. I'm privy to more information about her than you are, but I made a promise to Jaxson not to disclose it to anyone."

"Bullshit. If you're holding something back, spill it now, Atlas. If she's in danger, how the hell am I supposed to keep her safe?"

"Calm down, Maverick. What I can share is that I suspect she's keeping secrets from her brother regarding the reason for her visit. The nature of those secrets, only you can uncover from her. As for the other details… she'll have to reveal them herself. But when she does, keep an open mind, okay?"

"What the hell does that mean, Atlas?"

Atlas shook his head. "You and that hot head of yours are going to jeopardize something good. Remember, sometimes people keep secrets because they're afraid of being hurt."

Rory's phone vibrated in his pocket. Glancing at the screen as he retrieved it, he sighed. "That's Creed." He pressed the answer button. "Hey, everything okay?"

He left Kimber at the house with Creed, another member of LTI, knowing he needed to address his concerns with Atlas without her present. Creed was installing some cameras around the property, giving Rory an opportunity to discuss what was going on with Kimber. After waking up with her in his arms a few days ago, Rory realized he needed to unravel the mystery surrounding her, which felt more important than before. He was certain it was because, somehow, the captivating musician had stealthily captured his heart. The mere thought of her getting hurt left a bitter taste in his mouth.

"You need to get back here. A floral delivery was just made for your girl, and since then, she's locked herself in the master bedroom."

"What kind of delivery?" Rory's guard went up. A recollection stirred at the back of his mind from the first day he met her. She had received some flowers then and dismissed them. Now, he couldn't help but wonder if those flowers and the recent ones were connected.

"Flowers. She won't let me see what the card says, so I can only imagine it's not good."

"*Fuck.*" Rory growled into the phone. "I'll be there in twenty." Disconnecting, he stashed the device into his pocket. "I've got to go. It seems someone delivered flowers to Kimber, and whatever the note said had her rushing to her room. Creed says she's locked herself inside."

"I'll call the local florist and see what I can find." Davis stood and skirted the room.

"Go to her, Rory. See if she'll open up to you. Without knowing the complete story, we can't effectively help her. And starting from this moment forward, you're officially her protection, and Jaxson is the client. Which means you don't have to disclose it to her right now."

Rory held his boss' gaze for a moment, then nodded. Atlas seemed to be privy to something, but what? Rory had no idea. What hadn't Jaxson told him that Atlas knew? Rushing from the facility, Rory climbed into the car and headed in the direction of her house. He felt like Jaxson knew more than he had shared, so Rory decided calling his best friend was necessary. Uncertain if Jaxson would answer, given he was using his cell phone and not the satellite phone, Rory was surprised when Jaxson's voice came through the speaker.

"Maverick, what's up?"

"Cut the shit, Rory." Rory tried to contain his irritation, but it came out in his tone, anyway. "What does Atlas know about Kimber that I don't?"

"What are you talking about, Mav?" Jaxson sighed into the line. "Has something happened? Was I right... is Kimber keeping something from me?"

"Look, *Ice*," Rory hissed his name. "I don't know for sure, but there are a few things that aren't adding up. First, the explosion at the house, and now... well, she's been getting some weird notes. Almost stalkerish."

"What the fuck? Are you telling me my sister might have a stalker? Fuck, goddamn it."

"Whoa, calm down, brother. I said it was a possibility, not that we had a definite take on what's happening. We're still waiting for Hal to get the final report from the fire department on the explosion, and I'm digging into the flowers and notes. But if there is something about her you haven't shared, now is the time to come clean."

The oppressive silence lingered at the end of the phone, creating an atmosphere of tension that Rory found increasingly infuriating. He could almost feel Jaxson's contemplation on the other end, which only intensified Rory's growing frustration. The urgency of the situation demanded transparency, and if there were crucial details that could contribute to Kimber's protection, Rory expected Jaxson to lay everything bare.

As the seconds ticked away, Rory's mind traipsed back to the beautiful woman who was the center of their discussion. He grappled with the internal conflict of whether to disclose his own revelation to Jaxson. Rory was fairly sure he was falling for her. The weight of this revelation lingered on the tip of his tongue as he grappled with the decision to disclose the revelation to his best friend. The timing seemed fitting, considering the circumstances, yet a wariness of Jaxson's potential reaction held him back. The intricate dance of loyalty and confession played out in Rory's mind as he opted to keep this emotional tidbit concealed for the time being.

"Rory…" Jaxson took a deep breath, breaking the oppressive silence on the phone. "There's more to Kimber than she leads on.

Things she's kept hidden for good reason. But it's her place to reveal those things to you. I trust her to know when it's time to let you in, and I need you to do the same." His words held a weight of both concern and a brother's unwavering trust.

"Jaxson, if there's more to her story that could put her in danger, I need to know." Rory felt a mix of frustration and concern. "I want to protect her, but I can't do that effectively if I'm in the dark."

"I get it, Rory." Jaxson sighed, torn between loyalty to his sister and the desire to keep her safe. "But she's obviously going through something, and she's handling it in her own way. Kimber is stubborn to a fault, and we can't force her to open up. But we can be there for her. Monitor her, watch for any signs that something's amiss. Just don't push too hard. Whatever she's dealing with, it's obviously complicated, and pushing might make her shut down."

Disconnecting, Rory absorbed Jaxson's words. He knew his gut was right—Kimber was hiding more than she let on. The challenge now was finding a balance between respecting her privacy and ensuring her safety in a situation that seemed more intricate than he initially thought.

Guiding his car down the lengthy driveway, he parked and immediately noticed several vehicles, one of them marked with the insignia of the local fire department. The sight heightened his concern. He spotted Creed waving him over as he climbed out of the vehicle. A burning need to lay eyes on Kimber surged within him, driven by an instinct to ensure her safety. However, whatever Creed had to share was equally crucial. Rory trusted that Creed wouldn't have left Kimber alone without ensuring her well-being.

"Rory… she's been locked in her room since the flowers came. I didn't know what else to do. She's such a sweetheart. It makes me sick to think someone is playing around with her like this. Tried to get the note, but your girl is strong-willed. Told me in not so many words to mind my fuckin' business."

Rory couldn't help snorting a laugh at Creed's description. "Told you that, huh? And my girl? Seriously brother? This is Jaxson's sister… not my *woman*."

"Keep telling yourself that, Rory, but we can all see it, even if you can't. I'll be in back, talking to Hal. The fire investigator is 'round back with him. I'll go see what they've learned while you deal with that." He hooked a thumb over his shoulder toward the house. "Good luck."

Rory took the steps two at a time, the echoes of his footsteps resonating in the foyer. The house buzzed with activity as workers diligently cleaned up the aftermath of the damage. The air was thick with the scent of fresh paint and the rhythmic hum of power tools. Amid the construction sounds, a distant but distinct harmony reached Rory's ears—the soft strum of a guitar, accompanied by the melodic cadence of Kimber's voice. He navigated his way up the steps, each creaking beneath his weight, until he reached the threshold of the master bedroom.

Her voice carried through the wooden barrier, soft and smooth. His mind played the songs she sang in the bar, and goosebumps peppered his flesh. Kimber had a vocal talent capable of stirring deep emotions, a blend reminiscent of Rita Ora and Teddy Swims that washed over him. Gripping the doorknob, Rory slowly eased the door open, slipping inside and leaning against the frame. Unnoticed by Kimber, Rory stood there, captivated, watching her immerse herself in the music.

As she strummed the last chord, creating a tender melody that lingered in the air, Rory felt bound to break the silence. Clearing his throat, he spoke with genuine appreciation, "That was beautiful."

Kimber's head snapped up, and their gazes collided in a moment of shared vulnerability. She held his stare for a beat, her expressive eyes betraying emotions she desperately wanted to hide beneath the surface before blinking and breaking the connection. Shifting the guitar to the side, she blew out her breath.

"How long have you been standing there?"

"Long enough to know you've got mad skills, Kimber. Wanna tell me what sent you up here to lock yourself in the bedroom?"

"Just needed to work." Her response came with a casual deflection.

Rory arched a skeptical brow at her blatant lie. "And the flowers?"

Kimber stiffened briefly before a subtle surrender softened her demeanor.

"It's nothing. Just someone from Nashville who wants more than I am willing to give. You know how it is. I'm sure you've had plenty of women who can't take no for an answer. You're gorgeous, after all." She forced a grin, attempting to mask the weakness beneath humor.

Rory moved with deliberate steps, gracefully closing the distance between them. With a tender touch, he extended his hand, brushing the back of his knuckles gently across her cheek. The warmth of his palm cupped her face, the calloused yet gentle touch leaving a tingling sensation in its wake. His thumb traced a soothing pattern against her skin. A soft smile played on his lips, not just a mere gesture but a genuine expression aimed at dismantling the barriers of her defenses, inviting trust and openness. He wanted… no, needed her to *trust* him.

"Care to show me the note that came with them? Creed said you nearly passed out when you read whatever message the note held. Is that the reason you're here, Kimber? Was someone harassing you in Nashville? You know I can help you… no, I want to help you."

CHAPTER
TWELVE

"KIMBER, I know you're not telling me everything." Rory's expression softened, a mix of concern and frustration in his eyes. "It's clear something's troubling you. I want to help, but I can't if you keep shutting me out."

Kimber sighed, her gaze shifting to the cellphone, then back to Rory. The conflict within her was palpable. She wanted to trust him, to let him in, but years of guarding her secrets, her true self, made it almost impossible.

"I appreciate your concern, Rory, but some things are better left unsaid. Trust me, it's not as dramatic as it seems."

"Kimber, please trust me." Rory reached for her hand, his touch gentle yet filled with a silent plea for honesty. "Nashville, the flowers, the need for anonymity—it doesn't add up for just a songwriter. I'm not trying to pry, but if there's something you're running from or if someone's causing you trouble, I want to help."

Kimber felt a wave of anxiety wash over her as she sat there, the conflict within her growing more intense. The lies she had carefully crafted over time had always been her shield, protecting her from the world. But now, in Rory's presence, those very lies felt like a prison, suffocating her with their weight. She could feel the walls she had built around her heart, once a source of security, now closing in, making it hard to breathe.

Her gaze shifted to the phone, its insistent vibration on the wooden table a stark reminder of the reality she was trying to escape. The device seemed like a beacon, calling her to make a choice between continuing her façade or confronting the truth. She looked back at Rory, her eyes a turbulent sea of emotions—fear, guilt, longing, and a desperate wish for understanding.

The room felt smaller, the air thicker, as if every unspoken word between them added to the invisible barrier, Kimber felt trapped behind. Rory's gaze was filled with worry and confusion, his expression a mix of concern and a plea for honesty. Kimber's heart ached with the knowledge of the pain her secrets could cause, yet the fear of revealing her true self, of being helpless and exposed, held her back.

"I just… had a few uncomfortable encounters in Nashville. Overzealous fans for a small-time singer-songwriter, nothing more. I needed a break from all that, a place where no one knew me. That's why I'm here. And about the flowers, I think it's just someone not taking a hint that I'm not interested."

Rory studied her face, searching for the truth behind her words. "If you say so. Just know that I'm here for you, no matter what. You're not alone here."

Kimber offered a small, grateful smile, the turmoil inside her slightly eased by his words. Yet the shadows of her past loomed over her, a constant reminder of the life she left behind and the secrets she carried. As Rory's comforting presence surrounded her, she wondered how long she could keep the truth from him and what it would cost her when it finally came out.

Grabbing her phone, she shot him a smile and answered.

"Hey, Sophie. Whoa, whoa, slow down, honey." Rory immediately stiffened, moving closer to Kimber's body as she spoke. "What do you mean? Oh my God, Sophie… I'll be right there, sweetheart." Kimber stood and shoved the phone in her pocket. "Something's happened. We need to get to Sophie's."

"Whoa, darling." Rory grabbed her arm. "Slow down and tell me what she said."

"Please, Rory. I need to get to her *now*. She's the only friend I have in this town, and she needs me."

"Fine, but we're going to revisit *our* conversation later."

Kimber's heart pounded in her chest, her mind racing as much as her pulse. As she followed Rory out of the house, her thoughts were a whirlwind of worry and confusion. She glanced at him, noticing the deep lines of concern etched on his face. He was always so composed, but now there was a clear sense of urgency in his movements.

In the car, the tension was palpable. Rory's grip on the steering wheel was tight, his knuckles white. The usual hum of the engine and the passing scenery did little to calm Kimber's frayed nerves. She kept replaying Sophie's voice in her head, the fear and desperation that had trembled through the phone line.

"Kimber, you need to tell me what's going on." Rory broke the silence, his voice firm yet laced with worry. "What did Sophie say? Was it an accident? Is she hurt?"

Kimber turned to face him, her eyes glistening with unshed tears. "She was crying so hard, Rory. I couldn't make out everything. But she mentioned an accident and the police. That's all I know. I just… I have to be there for her."

The car sped through the streets, Rory navigating with a practiced ease despite the urgency. Kimber's thoughts were a tangle of fear for Sophie and anxiety over the secrets she still kept from Rory. She knew he was right. Their conversation wasn't over, but right now, her friend's crisis took priority over the complications of her own life.

"We're almost there, Kimber." Rory's voice broke through her thoughts again. "Whatever it is, we'll deal with it together. Okay?"

Kimber nodded, a small sense of solace in his promise. As they pulled up to Sophie's house, the sight of the police car deepened the knot of dread in her stomach. She braced herself, stepping out of the car and into the unknown.

The emotional intensity of the moment enveloped Kimber like a thick fog, her heart racing and her thoughts a chaotic whirlwind. Standing beside the Expedition, Rory's presence was both a comfort and a reminder of the gravity of the situation. Her fingers interlocked tightly with his, seeking solace in his touch. Her voice trembled as she spoke.

"Rory, what if it's Chloe? I can't..." Her voice lagged as she swallowed the fear burning in her throat.

Rory's eyes met hers, filled with a mixture of concern and determination. "Let's not jump to conclusions," he mumbled, trying to provide a steadying force amid uncertainty. He pulled out his phone and quickly dialed a number, his voice low and urgent. Kimber's heart hung on every word, the seconds stretching into what felt like hours.

As Rory talked, arranging for the possibility of support for Sophie and her family, Kimber's mind raced with images of Sophie's daughter, Chloe, whom she had heard so much about but had not yet met. The thought of something happening to the little girl was agonizing, twisting her stomach into knots.

Kimber listened as he spoke to someone on the other end. He filled them in on what little they knew and promised to call back with an update. He asked whoever it was to be on standby in the event Sophie and her husband needed something—especially if the incident involved her daughter.

Finally, a uniformed officer emerged, his approach causing Kimber's heart to skip a beat. "Are you Kimber?" he asked, his tone professional yet sympathetic. "Mrs. Reece is asking for you, Ma'am."

"Please, tell me what's going on." Kimber's voice was insistent, almost pleading, as she spoke with the officer. "Is Chloe hurt? Where's her dad… is it, Grady?" She could feel the tension in Rory's hand, a silent echo of her own anxiety.

The officer's response was a minor reprieve. "Her daughter is fine—confused and crying, but she isn't involved beyond that. Her father is in Montana on a fishing trip. My department is trying to get hold of him now." The words were a relief, yet they left so many questions unanswered.

Confusion clouded Kimber's face as she looked back at Rory, her eyes searching for some understanding. But the officer's next words shattered any semblance of calm.

"I'm afraid her husband was killed in an accident tonight."

The world seemed to stop for a moment.

"Oh, my God. Sophie." The name escaped Kimber's lips in a breathless whisper. In an instant, she released Rory's hand and ran toward the house, pushed by a surge of emotion. Her mind was a blur, filled with thoughts of Sophie's loss, the grief that must be consuming her friend.

Behind her, she heard Rory call her name, his voice tinged with concern, but Kimber couldn't stop, couldn't think. All she knew was that she needed to be with Sophie, to offer whatever comfort she could in the face of such crushing news. The steps to the house seemed to blur beneath her feet as she raced to be by her friend's side in this unimaginable moment of sadness.

Inside the living room, Kimber found Sophie sitting on the couch, her face etched with grief, a tiny figure huddled beside her. Chloe, just three years old, was nestled against her mother, her little sobs punctuating the heavy silence mingled with her mother's tears of pain. Sophie's eyes, red-rimmed and haunted, met Kimber's as she approached. Clutching Chloe closer, Sophie's voice broke as she whispered the devastating news.

"He's gone, Kimber. There was an accident, and… and he's dead."

Kimber's heart ached at the sight before her. She kneeled down, gently brushing a stray tear from Chloe's cheek. The child looked up, her gigantic eyes filled with confusion and fear. Kimber offered her a small, reassuring smile, trying to provide a sense of comfort if that was possible. Turning her attention back to Sophie, Kimber reached out, enveloping her friend in a supportive embrace.

"I'm here for you, Sophie," Kimber murmured softly. "Whatever you need, I'll take care of it. You're not alone." She shifted, so she was sitting beside her friend. "Do you need me to call anyone?" Sophie shook her head against Kimber's shoulder.

"No, the police have sent someone to notify Isaac's family. I'm sure this will somehow be my fault. They blame me for everything, anyway. Oh, God, Kimber. What am I going to do?"

In the subdued light of Sophie's living room, the atmosphere was heavy with sorrow. Sophie sat, almost lifeless, her eyes staring blankly at the space in front of her. Her silent sobs echoed off the frozen memories hanging framed against the painted backdrop. Rory had ordered dinner at some point, but Sophie refused to eat. Somehow, the man standing guard over them had got the toddler to eat a few bites. She was so young and had no idea the gravity of what was happening—Chloe only knew her mommy was crying. Kimber, sitting close by, reached out and took her friend's hand, squeezing it gently, breaking the calm silence that had finally descended from the room.

"Sophie," Kimber began, her voice soft yet filled with resolve. "I want to help with the funeral arrangements. You shouldn't have to worry about any of that right now. Just focus on you and Chloe."

Sophie nodded weakly, her voice barely audible. "Thank you, Kimber. I… I don't think I can—"

"Don't say another word," Kimber interrupted gently. "I'll take care of everything. Just try to eat something, okay?"

As the night wore on, Sophie's exhaustion became more clear. Her eyelids fluttered, struggling to stay open. Seeing this, Kimber turned to Rory, who had been a quiet yet comforting presence in the room. "Rory, could you help me get Sophie to bed? She needs to rest."

Without a word, Rory gently lifted Sophie, cradling her with a tenderness that spoke volumes of his character. Taking Chloe by the hand, Kimber led her to her bedroom, a colorful, cheerful space in stark contrast to the somber mood.

Kimber gently swept Chloe's hair back from her face as the little girl clambered into her lap. Chloe, seeking comfort, nestled her head against Kimber's shoulder, her small body trembling with the fragments of sobs. As Kimber wrapped her arms around Chloe, she felt a profound sense of protectiveness well up inside her. It was a natural maternal instinct, awakening in response to the child's vulnerability and need for comfort.

In the quiet of the room, with the soft glow of the nightlight casting a warm, gentle light, Kimber began to sing. Her voice was soft, a soothing balm to Chloe's distressed heart. The melody was simple yet beautiful, reminiscent of a lullaby, its notes floating through the room, weaving tranquility and peace.

The song was one of love and comfort, its rhythm steady and reassuring. As Kimber sang, her heart poured into each word, a silent promise to keep Chloe safe in that moment of heartache. The melody rose and fell, a soothing ebb and flow that seemed to wash away the relics of fear and sadness, replacing them with a sense of calm and safety.

Chloe's breathing slowly evened out, her small body relaxing against Kimber's as the song took effect. In that tender moment, the room was transformed into a sanctuary of safety.

CHAPTER
THIRTEEN

Outside the bedroom door, Rory stood motionless, his attention entirely captivated by the soft, melodic voice emanating from within. Kimber's singing seeped through the door, wrapping around him like a warm, comforting blanket. The lullaby was simple yet profoundly moving, each note resonating with a tenderness that touched a chord deep in his heart. He found himself captivated, not just by the beauty of the song, but by the kindness and love that Kimber exuded in this act of comfort.

The secrets she held, the mysteries that masked parts of her life, seemed to fade into the background at this moment. Standing there, immersed in the song's emotion, Rory felt a profound connection to Kimber, a realization dawning on him that he was falling in love with her. The revelation was both unexpected and overwhelming, stirring a deep emotional response. Rory felt a shift within himself, an acknowledgment of feelings that were growing stronger, more profound, and undeniably real. This unexpected epiphany, unfolding as he stood there, marked a turning point in his heart, one where affection surpassed the barriers of uncertainty and apprehension he felt, knowing there was more to the enigmatic woman on the other side of the door.

Rory was on the verge of stepping away, respecting Kimber's moment with Chloe, when the door swung open. Kimber stood there, a faint smile gracing her face even as tears glistened in her eyes.

"Hey," she greeted Rory, her voice carrying the unmistakable tremor of raw emotion. It was a simple word, but in the context of the evening's events, it held layers of meaning. It was a greeting, an acknowledgment of his presence, and perhaps a silent request for support.

Rory could hear the weariness in her voice, the strain of a night that had demanded so much from her emotionally. His concern immediately piqued, he reached out to her, his thumb gently brushing away a tear that had escaped down her cheek.

"You alright?" he asked softly, his eyes searching hers for a deeper understanding of her state. "What do you need?"

Kimber's response came with a sigh, heavy with the weight of the situation.

"For this to be a bad dream," she murmured. "That little girl in there… she's so confused. She knows her mommy is sad, and she can't understand why her daddy isn't here." Her voice broke a little, revealing the depth of her empathy for Chloe.

Rory observed Kimber closely, seeing the way her eyes glistened, a testament to her deep compassion. He understood that her empathy wasn't just a surface-level emotion. It was rooted in her own experiences, in the losses she had endured in her life. Kimber had lost her own parents when she was just a child, a parallel that made her particularly sensitive to Chloe's situation. This personal history gave her a unique perspective on the pain and the confusion that came with it, especially for someone so young.

Rory recognized not just the kindness in Kimber's heart but also the strength it took to face these emotions, to confront the echoes of her own past while trying to support those around her. Her empathy was a bridge, connecting her own past sorrows with the present challenges faced by Chloe and her mother. It was a testament to her resilience and her profound ability to connect with others, even in their darkest hours.

In response, Rory wrapped his arms around her, pulling her into a comforting embrace. He pressed a kiss to the top of her head, his gesture one of support and unity.

"It sucks," he admitted quietly. "But you're doing an amazing thing, Kimber. We're going to help them get through this."

Kimber's mind, ever racing in the face of crisis, suddenly jerked in his arms.

"I need to call her dad. I didn't even think about—" Her words were cut off as Rory gently placed his fingers over her lips, silencing her mid-sentence.

"I've already had Atlas look into it," he assured her, his voice calm. "They've arranged for him to be on a flight back home. He should be here by morning. For now, Kimber, there's nothing more you can do."

Kimber's eyes widened slightly in surprise and gratitude, a silent thank you communicated in her gaze.

"I assumed you'd want to stay here tonight, so Creed packed a small bag for us and dropped it off earlier while you were with Chloe." He stepped back, holding her hand, guiding her gently. "Let's go downstairs," he suggested. "We can work out a plan to help make things easier for Sophie. She's going to need all the support we can give."

As Kimber and Rory descended the staircase, there was a solemn unity between them, a shared commitment to offer all the support they could muster. Kimber, feeling the weight of the night's events, let herself sink into the couch, drawing her knees close to her chest in a self-protective embrace. Rory settled beside her, his arm extended along the back of the couch, a silent offer of comfort.

"What are you thinking?" Rory gently probed. His voice was soft, inviting her to share her thoughts.

Kimber's shoulder gave a slight shrug, her gaze distant as she delved into her past.

"I remember the night my parents died. When we found out they weren't coming home… I just wanted to disappear. My brother Jaxson, he was so angry, he punched holes in the wall." Her voice wavered slightly, the memory vivid and painful. "But then, my aunt, the same woman who would become our guardian, just walked up to Jaxson and embraced him. She whispered something to him, and it was like watching someone defuse a bomb. What he did next…" Kimber paused, lost in the recollection.

Rory, feeling the intensity of her emotions, placed his hand on her leg, gently interlacing their fingers. Kimber looked down at their entwined hands, a faint smile touching her lips despite the sadness in her eyes.

"What did he do?" Rory asked, coaxing her back from the memories.

Kimber exhaled, her eyes still tinged with the ghosts of the past.

"He stood up straight, came over to me, and pulled me into a hug. He told me, with such conviction, that no matter what, he'd always have my back. I completely broke down then, even more than before. I was only ten, and Jaxson, he was seventeen, a senior in high school. At that moment, he was more than a brother; he was my hero. And when he saw that I couldn't shake off the grief, he suggested an outlet to help me cope. It was my aunt who introduced me to music. The piano… it became my sanctuary, my way of coping. It was where I could express everything I couldn't put into words."

Kimber's muscles tensed noticeably, a reaction that seemed almost involuntary as the topic of the damaged piano surfaced. It wasn't just any instrument; it was the very piano that had offered her solace in her darkest times, a haven during the painful journey after loss. Sensing her distress, Rory tried to reassure her with gentle words.

"Hey… I told you we'd do what we could to get it fixed."

She began to respond, "I know—" but her reply was abruptly interrupted. A sudden, sharp cry shattered their conversation, slicing through the tense atmosphere like a knife. It was Sophie's voice, unmistakable and filled with distress.

Instantly springing into action, Kimber leaped from her seat and dashed up the staircase. Her heart pounded with a mix of concern and urgency. At the top, she found Chloe, her eyes wide with alarm, rooted to the spot outside her mother's bedroom. Without a moment's hesitation, Rory scooped up the little girl, holding her close.

"I got you, Sophie," Kimber whispered, her voice a soothing balm during the chaotic night as she reached Sophie's bedside.

Rory watched silently, a mixture of concern and helplessness in his eyes. Chloe, still in his arms, squirmed, her body language a silent plea to join her mother. Understanding the unspoken request, Kimber nodded slightly, making room on the bed. Gently, Rory placed Chloe down, tucking the covers snugly around the trio. Then, with a tenderness that seemed to come naturally to him, Rory leaned in and pressed a soft kiss to Kimber's temple, a silent gesture of tenderness.

"I'll sleep in Chloe's bedroom," he murmured quietly, his voice steady despite the night's disruptions. "Call out if you need something. Her dad should be here in the morning. After that, we can figure out what's next."

He left the room quietly, allowing Kimber, Sophie, and Chloe the peace they needed in the darkened room. Rory's steps were soft as he made his way downstairs, a thoughtful expression on his face. He found the bags Creed had thoughtfully brought over earlier and carefully picked them up, his movements precise. As he ascended the stairs once again, his mind was a whirlwind of thoughts.

Reaching the room where he would spend the night, Rory flicked on the bedside lamp. The room was instantly bathed in a warm, yellow glow, casting long shadows across the walls and creating a cozy, if not slightly cramped, atmosphere. He couldn't help but snort at the absurdity of the situation—him, a grown man, preparing to sleep in a bed clearly meant for someone much smaller. The spare bedroom was out of the question, filled as it was with boxes and devoid of a bed. The couch downstairs was another option he swiftly discarded. It was essential to be close to Kimber and the girls, to be there for them at a moment's notice, especially considering the unresolved questions of Kimber's secret admirer that lingered in the air.

The mystery of who had sent Kimber the token of unwanted affection was still unsolved, a nagging worry at the back of his mind. If Kimber was in any kind of danger, Rory knew he couldn't afford to let his guard down, even for a moment. This protective instinct drove him to choose the inconvenient but necessary option of the twin bed.

After a moment of contemplation, Rory stripped off his shirt and pants, settling for comfort in an unfamiliar bed. He wriggled beneath the covers, shifting and turning until he found a position that was somewhat comfortable, given the circumstances. His last action before attempting to sleep was to check his phone, scrolling through text messages. He noted updates from Atlas, Creed, and Davis, his trusted team, who were tirelessly working to unravel the mystery surrounding Kimber. Rory had full confidence in their abilities; if there was something to be found, they would undoubtedly uncover it. While he was new working with the men, he knew, based on their history in the military, they wouldn't give up until they had answers. And no matter what they found, they would undoubtedly have his back. Working for LTI was far better than babysitting Hollywood's spoiled population.

Finally, allowing the exhaustion and the weight of the night's events to overtake him, Rory closed his eyes. He drifted into a light, restless sleep, his senses still alert. He was ready to wake at the slightest sound, prepared to respond if Kimber or the girls needed him. At that moment, under the soft glow of the bedside lamp, Rory's presence was a silent vow of protection and vigilance, even as sleep claimed him.

CHAPTER
FOURTEEN

KIMBER WASN'T SURPRISED to find Rory downstairs in the kitchen. He glanced over his shoulder and smiled at her and Chloe. Chloe had woken up earlier than both Kimber and Sophie, disrupting the quiet morning with the energy only a young child could muster. Kimber had risen, finding a thoughtful gesture from Rory—a fresh set of clothes laid out for her, accompanied by a note suggesting they meet downstairs.

As they entered the kitchen, Chloe eagerly released Kimber's hand and sprinted toward a familiar figure. "Pops," she called out joyfully, throwing herself into the arms of Grady Reece, Sophia's father.

Grady's face was etched with worry, but it softened as he embraced his granddaughter, showering her with affectionate kisses. He wore an expression of deep concern as he pressed kisses to her head. "Hey, bean. How are you?"

"Pops, where's Daddy?" Chloe's innocent question about her father brought a heavy silence. "Did you bring him with you?"

The quick intake of breath had Kimber turning to her friend in the doorway. "Sophie."

Kimber's friend's presence added another layer of emotion to the already charged atmosphere. Sophie's pained expression prompted Kimber to move toward her, but Sophie signaled her to stop when she held her hand up, halting her movement. She instead went straight to her father, seeking comfort in his embrace.

"He's gone, Daddy… Isaac, he's gone," she uttered, her voice laced with grief.

Grady enveloped both his daughters in a tight hug, his response simple yet filled with understanding. "I know, princess. I know."

FEELING like an outsider in this intimate family moment, Kimber gestured to Rory, indicating they should give the family some privacy. After offering Sophie a supportive hug and assuring Grady they were available if needed, Kimber and Rory quietly exited, heading toward his SUV.

The ride was filled with a palpable emotional tension. Kimber, lost in her thoughts, finally broke the silence, expressing her gratitude to Rory.

"Thank you, Rory. You didn't have to help Sophie and Chloe, but you did."

"I'll do anything for you, Kimber." Rory's response was immediate and heartfelt as he intertwined his fingers with hers. "I hope you realize this thing between us isn't just a fling."

Kimber, conflicted and emotional, started to respond but was interrupted by Rory's understanding words.

"Don't. Not now, Kimber. I know you have a life in Nashville. And when it comes time for you to go back, we can figure this thing between us out then. For now, let's just focus on the here and now and help your friend through this rough period."

The mention of Nashville sparked a reminder in Kimber's mind. "Shit. I need to make a call."

Kimber's realization about needing to contact Avery was a stark reminder of her life outside the current turmoil. She'd been inadvertently neglecting her friendship with Avery, the third member of their close-knit trio since childhood. This avoidance wasn't just about being preoccupied; it was also about evading a reality Kimber wasn't ready to face.

Rory, sensing the importance of the call, offered his phone. "Here, use mine."

Kimber took it with a moment of hesitation, appreciating the gesture. She dialed Avery's number, a sequence so familiar, it was almost automatic. The phone barely rang before Avery's voice erupted from the other end—a mix of anger and worry.

"What in the fuck, Kimber?" she exclaimed. "I've been calling and texting you for fucking weeks. If it wasn't for Henley talking to Jaxson, I'd have gotten in my car to come down there and make sure you weren't dead… or worse, missing."

Kimber winced at the harshness in Avery's voice, feeling a pang of guilt.

"I know. I'm sorry… look," she began, her eyes flicking to Rory, who was observing the conversation with obvious interest. She was careful with her words, conscious of his presence. "I ran into Sophie when I got here. She and I have been reconciling, and I just wanted to pretend—" She cut herself off abruptly, throwing Rory a glance that silently pleaded for him to have missed her words.

Avery's tone softened, understanding creeping into her voice. "Awe, Kimber… you can't run from this, but I won't lecture you. How's Sophie? I miss her and hate that we lost touch."

In response, Kimber recounted the events that had unfolded since her arrival in Alabama, though she carefully omitted the details about the threats she had received. She knew Avery well enough to predict her reaction. Sure enough, Avery promised to be there later that day. She wanted to be there for Kimber, to see Sophie, and to offer her support in any way she could.

The call ended with Kimber feeling a mixture of relief and apprehension. Avery's impending visit was both a comfort and a reminder of the complications awaiting her in her personal life. Kimber was acutely aware of the balancing act she was performing between her past and her present and the looming decisions she would soon have to face.

She handed him back his phone, which he stowed in his pocket.

"Thanks. Looks like you're going to meet my bestie, Avery. She and her man, Henley, are coming down. They'll be here tonight. I guess we need to make sure the spare room is usable," she said, trying to maintain a semblance of normalcy despite the recent upheavals.

As they pulled up to the house, Kimber stepped out of the SUV, her mind preoccupied with thoughts of Avery's visit. However, her movements abruptly halted as she caught sight of something disturbing at the top of the porch steps. There, cruelly displayed on the wooden planks, was the remains of her guitar, a beloved possession now rendered useless. A sharp intake of breath escaped her as shock and disbelief gripped her.

"Fuck." Rory immediately stepped forward, positioning himself protectively between Kimber and the wreckage of her guitar. He pulled out his phone and dialed quickly. "We have a situation. I need you at Kimber's," he spoke into the phone, his voice laced with urgency. Turning to Kimber, his expression grave, he instructed firmly, "Darling, I need you to get back in the SUV and lock the doors." His eyes scanned the area, a curse slipping from his lips as he noticed something else.

Kimber's gaze followed his, and she gasped in horror at the sight of her car. It was defaced with hateful words and menacing threats. The reality of her situation suddenly became starkly clear—the threats she had received were no longer just words. They were manifesting into tangible, frightening acts of violence. A wave of fear washed over her, not just for herself, but for Rory, too.

"What about you? I don't want you hurt... please, Rory," she pleaded, her voice tinged with panic. The thought of him coming to harm was unbearable, as unrealistic as it was. Rory was a former Navy SEAL. She knew he could take care of himself, but the notion of 'what if' left her consumed with paralyzing fear.

Rory, however, remained focused on the task at hand.

"Sweetheart, I need to check the house. Whoever did this got inside," he said, his tone conveying both his concern for her safety and his determination to secure the premises. "And could still be inside."

Kimber nodded, her voice barely above a whisper, laden with a haunting fear. "I don't want my monsters to hurt you," she confessed, her words hinting at hidden troubles.

Rory stepped closer, his presence reassuring yet filled with concern. He gently cupped her jaw, his touch a mix of protection and inquiry.

"What monsters, Kimber?" he asked, his voice soft yet firm, seeking to understand the depth of her fears.

"I can't tell you about the monsters under my bed, Rory." Kimber's eyes, filled with a vulnerability she rarely showed, met his. "You won't look at me the same." A single tear escaped, tracing a path down her cheek, a symbol of her inner turmoil and the secrets she held close.

"You can tell me anything, Kimber. I'm not afraid of the monsters under the bed. I'm afraid of a world where I'm not there to chase them away for you. But to chase them away… I need to know all your secrets."

Their moment of intense connection was abruptly interrupted by the sound of tires crunching on gravel. Rory's hand fell away as they both turned to see Atlas, Creed, and two other men emerge from a blacked-out SUV.

"Thanks for coming. I haven't checked inside," Rory said, addressing the newly arrived team as he gestured toward the house. "Did the cameras catch anything?"

Kimber watched as one of the men, leaning casually against the hood of the truck, shook his head. "No, they somehow got them offline before getting close enough to get caught on them."

The revelation added another layer of concern to the situation. The deliberate sabotage of the cameras showed a calculated and forethought plan by someone who knew how to evade their security measures. It wasn't just a random act of vandalism; it was a targeted attack. Kimber couldn't help but feel a growing sense of dread at the realization. The 'monsters' she feared were proving to be all too real, and now Rory and his team were drawn into the fray.

Kimber's world seemed to tilt on its axis as Atlas addressed her, his tone serious and concerned. But before he could say more, Rory's protective growl cut through the air, a clear sign of his instinct to shield Kimber from further distress. Atlas, undeterred yet cautious, shifted his gaze between Kimber and Rory.

"You need to tell him, sweetheart. It's time. We can't help you without knowing what's going on," he urged gently, emphasizing the need for transparency.

Kimber, confusion etched on her face, struggled to grasp the implications of Atlas's words.

"Wait… what are you talking about?" she asked, her brow furrowing as she tried to piece together the puzzle. Then, like a jigsaw falling into place, it dawned on her. "*Jaxson.*" She said her brother's name with such disgust, it made Rory wine. "You didn't need a place to stay, did you?" A wave of realization and hurt crashed over her. She closed her eyes, overwhelmed by the sense of betrayal. "You were here because he didn't believe my reasons for coming home. This whole thing was a cover to make sure I was guarded."

Her accusation hung in the air, heavy with implications. The idea that her return home was under scrutiny, that her every move was being monitored under the guise of a friend needing somewhere to stay, and that what transpired between them was a ruse was a bitter pill to swallow.

Rory, sensing Kimber's pain, stepped closer. His hand rested on her shoulder, and his eyes conveyed a mix of concern, empathy, and a readiness to defend himself, whatever the truth might be. This moment was a turning point, a realization that the situation was more complex and perilous than she had initially thought. It was a time for truths to be revealed and for veils of pretense to be lifted. Only then could they truly confront the threats lurking in the shadows. Knowing her next words would be a bullet to his heart, she took a deep breath and pulled out of his hold. Kimber's revelation was heavy with the weight of a truth long concealed.

"Jaxson was right. I came home to hide from a stalker—one who made several death threats. I didn't want the circus of the media to hear about it, so I thought coming here would give it time to die down and maybe go away. I was wrong, and now, whoever it is, has found me."

Rory, his expression a mix of surprise and concern, glanced at his friends. They all shared his confusion, except for Atlas, whose face bore an expression of understanding and sympathy.

"I don't understand. I thought you were just a songwriter," Rory said, trying to reconcile this latest information with what he knew about Kimber.

"Ha. I am a songwriter but haven't written for myself in nearly a decade." Kimber's response was tinged with bitterness. "You were right when you told me musicians sell their souls to a label when they sign. I wish I knew that when I signed mine over."

Rory's confusion deepened. "Signed yours over… I don't understand."

With a sense of finality, Kimber pulled open the door to the SUV, pausing as she looked back at Atlas, who gave her a nod of encouragement. She closed her eyes, bracing herself for the pain her next words would cause. She was about to shatter the illusion of the life she had been living.

"Kimber…" Rory began, stepping toward her, but she stopped him with a shake of her head.

Then, unexpectedly, she began to sing through her tears, her voice breaking with emotion she couldn't hide even if she tried.

I'm gonna be a star, lighting up the night,

With my heart on my sleeve and my dreams taking flight,

I'll reach for the sky 'til I'm shining from afar,

In this cosmic symphony, I'm gonna be a star.

THE SOUND of the SUV door closing behind her was a stark finality, a symbolic closure to the façade she had maintained. Through the tinted glass, she watched as a tumult of emotions crossed Rory's face. Atlas moved to comfort him, but Rory jerked away from the touch. Atlas' hand fell to his side as he muttered something inaudible. Rory, fists clenched, spun on his heel and headed toward the house, his reaction a clear indication of the inner turmoil Kimber's revelation had caused.

Kimber sat inside the SUV, a profound ache in her chest. She had just exposed a part of herself she had kept hidden, opening up a chasm between her and Rory. The pain of the moment was palpable, a mixture of regret, fear, and a deep sense of vulnerability. She had laid bare her truth, and now she could only watch as Rory grappled with the reality of her confession.

CHAPTER
FIFTEEN

I'M GONNA BE A STAR, lighting up the night,

With my heart on my sleeve and my dreams taking flight,

I'll reach for the sky 'til I'm shining from afar,

In this cosmic symphony, I'm gonna be a star.

The words struck Rory with the force of a gunshot, reverberating through his very core. The sight of her tears cascading down her cheeks like relentless, never-ending rivers, seared into his soul with the intensity of an uncontrolled wildfire. It was a song he had heard countless times, a melody so familiar yet now so painfully heartbreaking. He remembered sharing his complicated feelings about it with her, confiding in the car how he, oddly enough, hated to love it. The song, symbolic of the very type of superstar he loathed, now echoed with a newfound irony.

The soft touch of someone's hand rested on his shoulder. "You need to remember who she was before telling you the truth." Rory shrugged out of Atlas's hold and clenched his fists as his friend continued. "She had her reasons for keeping it secret."

Secret.

Funny how secrets seemed to be the norm in her family. Jaxson, his best friend, had never disclosed the truth about his sister. All this time, Rory had believed she was just another ambitious songwriter trying to carve her path in Nashville's competitive music scene.

Turning on his heel, Rory cast a final, lingering glance at the darkened windows of the SUV, a silent witness to the unfolding drama. His voice, steady but laced with a hint of command, broke the heavy air.

"Someone, watch the car. I'm clearing the house." He moved away swiftly, practically running from his boss or, more accurately, from the woman who now seemed to mock him from behind the glass at a distance.

His thoughts were a tumultuous mix of anger and disdain. He despised people like her, those who wore masks of charm and charisma. His time in Los Angeles had given him more than his fair share of encounters with spoiled rockstars, and the realization that he had fallen in love with someone akin to them left a bitter taste in his mouth. He *hated* people like her. And now… he'd gone and fallen in love with one of them.

As Rory ascended the steps to the house, a somber pause overtook him. He squatted down beside the shattered remains of what used to be an instrument, a silent witness to the turmoil unfolding around them. The broken strings and splintered wood told a story of violence, but it was the image attached to it that truly captured his attention. It was a picture of Kimber, or rather, the persona she had so carefully crafted and now was desperately trying to conceal. Her face, once vibrant and full of life, was now marred with a crudely drawn circle and a harsh slash through it. The words scrawled beneath the image sent a chilling wave through him.

Too bad it's not your funeral you're planning. No worries… yours will be soon enough. You took my life—now I'll take yours.

Despite the burning anger coursing through him, Rory couldn't suppress a shiver. The threat was menacing, personal, and it brought a sense of urgency to protect Kimber, even from a distance, from the twisted individual behind this message.

His thoughts were interrupted as Davis approached, his presence suddenly grounding.

"Atlas and Creed went inside. Here," Davis said, offering a plastic bag and some gloves. "Let's bag that. The police are on their way."

Rory's mind, however, was elsewhere. "Where's Kimber?" he asked, his gaze sweeping the yard anxiously.

"She's locked inside the vehicle. She's safe, Rory," Davis assured him. "You know, she's nothing like what I expected Stormer Heart to be. That's an act, a mask she wears for the crowd. And honestly, had she not told us who she was, I'd have never guessed it. Kimber is the complete opposite of Stormer, in looks and in personality."

But Rory's mind was entrenched in his own preconceived notions. "Doesn't matter," he muttered, slipping on the glove Davis handed him and carefully placing the threatening note inside the bag. "I hate people like her."

"Pretty bold statement, Rory. Not all *famous* people are bad. And I suspect her being here is more than a stalker."

Rory's actions were systematic as he sealed the evidence away, but his thoughts were turbulent. Davis's words echoed in his mind, challenging his deep-seated prejudices and forcing him to confront the complex layers of Kimber's identity. The situation was more than a mere confrontation with a stalker; it was a revelation of the intricate façade of who she truly was. The divide between Kimber and Stormer Heart, as Davis pointed out, was vast and complicated, adding another dimension to Rory's already conflicted feelings. He was in love with Kimber… but could he love Stormer Heart? He didn't think he could. Everything she stood for made his skin crawl.

"Why do you hate celebrities so much?" Davis asked, taking the evidence bag from Rory. His tone was not accusatory, but genuinely curious. "Bodyguard gigs are just that—gigs. Why let the actions of others sway you from something that could be good for you?"

"I've seen what famous people can do to others." Rory felt a pang in his chest as he thought about his sister. "My sister almost took her life over something a rich celebrity did. Because of her money and fame, the whole situation was just brushed under the rug. I almost lost my sister because someone had deep pockets and was in the spotlight. I won't give my heart to someone like that, Davis. I can't risk it."

He closed his eyes, haunted by the memory of the phone call that had come when he was miles away, across the ocean. His sister, Roslyn, had been so full of hope and excitement only weeks before when they'd talked. An actress from Hollywood had shown interest in her fashion designs. But the excitement had turned to ashes when the truth came out—the actress had claimed Roslyn's designs as her own. Roslyn lost everything, including her sense of self.

Rory's parents, both teachers, did what they could, but their resources paled compared to the wealth of the actress. Faced with the prospect of a legal battle that would bankrupt her family or walking away from her dreams, Roslyn had chosen the latter. She spiraled into a deep depression afterward, a fall that took her years to climb back from. She was better now, living in the present, but Rory couldn't forget how a rich, spoiled celebrity had nearly destroyed his sister's life.

His train of thought was broken by the sound of an approaching vehicle. Rory watched as a large truck pulled up, and a tiny, energetic woman hopped out, heading their way. He was about to call out when the door of the SUV, where Kimber was locked inside, burst open.

"Avery!" Kimber's voice cut through the air.

Kimber rushed from the backseat, leaving the door wide open. Avery, the woman from the truck, turned just in time as Kimber reached her. In a moment filled with raw emotion, Kimber enveloped Avery in a tight embrace, almost knocking her over with the intensity of her reaction upon seeing her friend.

This scene, unfolding before Rory's eyes, offered a stark contrast to his own internal turmoil. The genuine affection between Kimber and Avery was palpable, challenging the rigid perceptions he held about celebrities and their world. At this moment, Kimber wasn't Stormer Heart, the famous persona—she was just a woman, relieved and grateful to see her friend. It made Rory question himself, even as he stood there, conflicted and unsure.

An older man emerged from the driver's side, his head shaking as he approached Kimber. Rory, caught in a moment of jealousy, advanced toward the two women. His feelings, though irrational, momentarily clouded his judgment. Kimber stood on her tiptoes and pressed a kiss to the man's cheek before turning toward Rory and the others.

Kimber ignored Rory as she turned to face his boss. "Atlas, let me introduce you to my best friend, Avery Downs."

"Actually, it's Sparks," Avery corrected with a bright smile, her eyes playfully darting to Kimber. "We sort of eloped."

Kimber's reaction was immediate and loud. "What?" she screeched, a mix of shock and mock outrage in her voice. "You got married without me? Henley, what the hell?" She playfully slapped his arm, displaying the affectionate bond he imagined she shared with him. It was something he was curious about for sure.

Avery bit her lip, her face awash with a mix of guilt and happiness as she faced Kimber. Henley, clearly a man of few words but strong actions, drew Avery closer against his bulky frame.

"Kimber, be mad at me," he said calmly. "I wasn't willing to wait to make her mine—not when she's carrying my baby."

"Holy shit." Kimber gasped. "You're pregnant? Oh my God, Avery." Kimber grabbed her friend, wrapping an arm around both Avery and Henley. "Should you even be here?"

Avery gently extricated herself from Kimber's hold, laughing. "I'm pregnant, not invalid. And I'm just a few weeks along, so… yeah. I should be here." Her laughter was infectious, lightening the mood. But then Avery's eyes took in the surrounding scene, her expression changing from joy to confusion. "Wait… who are all these guys? What's going on, Kimber?" Her tone was a mix of curiosity and concern, highlighting her sudden realization that she had walked into a situation far more complex than a simple reunion.

"Mr. and Mrs. Sparks, can we take this inside? We can explain everything there. Being out here makes the scene more volatile," Rory suggested, his voice carrying a mix of urgency and concern.

Henley, protective and alert, stiffened at Rory's words. "Is it happening here, Kimber?" he asked, his voice laced with worry, revealing his awareness of the situation.

Rory couldn't hide his surprise. "You know about her stalker?" he asked, his voice a low growl.

"Yeah, I'm her head of security," Henley replied, his expression serious. "And against my advice to go public with this, she came home for a 'break.'" He emphasized the word 'break' with air quotes, his frustration evident. "But she was supposed to let me know if that plan changed."

"Seems like she's good at keeping secrets," Rory muttered, unable to keep the bitterness from his tone.

His words struck a chord, Kimber visibly wincing at the accusation. Rory felt a pang of regret at seeing her reaction. He hated that his words hurt her, yet he couldn't shake off his own pain from the revelation that she wasn't who he thought she was. Amid this tension, Avery, ever perceptive, linked her arm with

Kimber's and gently led her across the yard. Rory watched them, his gaze lingering on Kimber. Despite his efforts to harbor resentment, his heart was in conflict, struggling against his attempts to hate her.

"You're in love with her," Henley's voice abruptly pulled Rory back to the present.

"What?" Rory turned, meeting Henley's scrutinizing gaze.

"Kimber… you love her," Henley stated plainly, as if reading Rory's innermost feelings.

"Doesn't matter." Rory shook his head, denying the truth he wasn't ready to face. "It won't work. She lied to me about who she is. I don't date celebrities. Rich people have a way of destroying lives."

"Wow, you're a cynical bastard, aren't you?" Henley's response was blunt, almost challenging.

Rory bristled at the accusation. "Excuse me?"

Henley didn't back down. "You've got this preconceived notion of what she should be like. But let me tell you something," he said, his voice firm. "That woman inside is the furthest thing from a snobby, rich girl. She has a heart of gold and always puts others first. That's why she lets the label push her around, singing the pop songs you hear on the radio. Her band would be nothing without those tracks, and she knows it. Instead of playing what she wants, she sacrifices her artistic desires to keep them afloat."

Henley's words offered a unique perspective on Kimber, painting her not as a deceitful celebrity but as a selfless individual caught in the complexities of the music industry. His description of Kimber clashed starkly with Rory's preconceptions, challenging him to reconsider his stance and to see Kimber in a new light— not just as Stormer Heart, the superstar, but as Kimber, the person with a heart of gold hidden beneath the glitz and glamor.

Reluctantly, Rory trudged inside the house, his mind still wrestling with the revelations and Henley's words. Inside, the atmosphere was a blend of urgency and controlled chaos. Atlas swiftly briefed Henley on the latest developments regarding Kimber's stalker, ensuring that everyone was on the same page. Meanwhile, Davis took charge of liaising with the police, meticulously ensuring that a detailed report was filed in the event the situation escalated.

Once the three of them left, promising to return the next day to help with Sophie, Kimber's friend, Rory couldn't help but feel that they were only experiencing the lull before a more significant disruption. The phrase "when it rains, it pours" echoed in his mind, aptly describing the cascade of events they were ensnared in. Rory felt like he was caught in the eye of this emotional and psychological storm. He wasn't ignorant of the fact that the coming days were unpredictable. His time in the

Army taught him that. It didn't matter how much you prepared for something… storms raged with an unpredictability that left chaos in its wake.

And Rory's gut said the storm that sat on the horizon threatened to change everything.

CHAPTER
SIXTEEN

KIMBER AVOIDED RORY SUCCESSFULLY, but the funeral for her closest friend's husband would prevent that from happening. The inevitable of being in proximity to Rory was about as real as her best friend being pregnant. Since coming home, Avery had gone to the doctor. Henley insisted when she became ill after eating dinner one night. As silly as it was, he refused to take a chance on her—with his history of losing his wife to cancer, Kimber couldn't blame him.

Kimber's smile faded as soon as she saw Sophie descending the stairs, dressed in somber black, with little Chloe's hand in hers.

Kimber crouched down to Chloe's level, gently brushing the strawberry blonde locks from her face. "How you doing, kiddo?" she asked, her voice soft and caring.

Chloe shrugged. She was only three and likely didn't truly grasp what was happening. She only knew that her mom was sad, and her dad wasn't coming home.

"Okay, Aunt KK," she replied, using the nickname she had affectionately given Kimber. "Mommy is sad, though. She said we're going to see Daddy today, that he has to go away for a long time. Why, Auntie KK? Why does Daddy have to leave?"

"Sometimes, parents have to go away, squirt." Kimber's heart ached as she responded, trying to explain in terms a child might understand. "Mine had to take the same trip when I was a little older than you."

"Did they come back?" Chloe asked innocently.

Kimber closed her eyes, swallowing the pain. "No, baby girl, they didn't. But I know I'll see them again one day. And guess what? I bet your daddy, and my parents are together, watching over us and smiling at how beautiful you are. Come on," she encouraged, standing up. "Spin around and show me your dress."

Chloe, in her black tutu, had been Kimber's special project. When Sophie nearly broke down at her daughter's insistence on the skirt, Kimber had used her connections to fulfill the little girl's wish.

Sophie, grateful yet somber, whispered a thank you to Kimber. "And don't think we aren't going to talk about you being *Stormer Heart*," she added.

"I know, Soph." Kimber sighed, her gaze drifting to Rory, who stood silently beside the SUV. "And I'm really sorry I didn't tell you. I hate who she is—Stormer has cost me so much." Her eyes lingered on Rory for a moment longer. "I don't think I'm going back to Nashville."

At that moment, Kimber stood at a crossroads, her heart torn between the life she had known as Stormer Heart and the real existence she yearned for. The presence of Rory, the man she'd deceived, served as a stark reminder of the price of her fame. Her decision to potentially leave Nashville was not solely about escaping a persona. It was about searching for a semblance of truth in a life that had become increasingly defined by facades.

"That's big, Kimber. Does he know?" she asked, gesturing subtly toward Rory.

"No." Kimber shook her head, a mix of resignation and sadness in her eyes. "He won't even look at me, much less listen to my apology."

"You're wrong about that, Kimber. He might say one thing… but the way he looks at you says something different. And from someone who sees how fleeting life can be, don't miss the chance of having love."

With those words echoing in her mind, Kimber wrapped an arm around Sophie, gently guiding her toward the SUV. Rory, ever the professional despite the emotional turmoil, opened the door for them. Chloe was strapped securely in her car seat between

Kimber and Sophie as they made their way to the funeral home. The drive was quiet, reflective, giving Kimber time to think about the whirlwind of change that had swept through her life in the past two months.

Since returning home, Kimber's perspective on her life and career had shifted dramatically. The allure of the limelight had faded, replaced by a longing for authenticity and genuine connections. In the last three days alone, she had found joy in simple moments with Avery, Sophie, and Chloe, like teaching Chloe how to strum a guitar. These experiences felt more real to her than any concert or fan meeting.

Kimber had also found inspiration in this return to her roots, penning a new song that deviated significantly from her usual pop hits. It was the kind of music she had always wanted to write, a stark contrast to the glitzy, manufactured image of Stormer Heart.

Now, as she sat in the SUV, heading toward a solemn occasion, Kimber couldn't help but feel like Stormer Heart was on her way to her funeral. A character covered in makeup and lies. The realization that she no longer wanted to be part of that world was both liberating and daunting. It was a step toward finding her true self, even if it meant leaving behind the fame and success she had known. Yet Rory and the unresolved feelings between them added a complication to her thoughts. Sophie's words lingered in her mind, a reminder that amidst the turmoil, there might still be a chance for something genuine. If only she could find the courage to reach out and tell him that she was in love with him.

Soon enough, the service was over, and they were once again ushered into the vehicle. Kimber, feeling an unsettling sense of being watched, cast her eyes out the window, scanning the surrounding trees. Finding nothing amiss, she focused back on the task at hand, helping little Chloe out of the car.

As they approached the site, Chloe eagerly ran to her grandparents, Isaac's parents, who stood somewhat aloof from the rest. Sophie, wiping away her tears, expressed her reluctance at their presence.

"Wonderful. I was hoping they wouldn't show," she murmured, a hint of distress in her voice.

Kimber, familiar with dealing with high-society types from her Nashville days, reassured Sophie with a protective edge to her words. "Don't worry, I won't let them act like assholes."

Sophie's brief laugh in response was a small reprieve from her grief. Pausing, she turned to Kimber with a request. "Will you do me a favor?"

"Anything," Kimber replied, offering her friend a supportive embrace as they moved toward Avery and the others.

"Will you sing 'One More Day'?" Sophie asked, her voice laced with a deep need for comfort.

Kimber hesitated, not wanting to draw attention to herself, but seeing the sincerity in Sophie's eyes, she knew this was more than a simple request. It was a plea for solace in a moment of profound sorrow. Nodding in agreement, Kimber prepared herself to sing the old but familiar Diamond Rio song.

As everyone gathered around the flower-covered casket, the pastor began his words, filling the air with messages of hope and remembrance. The scent of roses wafted through the air, a touching backdrop to the pastor's comforting words and the collective sorrow of those present.

When the pastor concluded with a prayer, Sophie gave Kimber a small, grateful nod. Kimber took out her phone, carefully adjusting the volume before the soft chords of Dimond Rio's "One More Day" began to play. With a deep breath, Kimber allowed the lyrics to flow from her, her voice carrying the poignant melody, saturating the air with a mix of sadness, reminiscence, and an underlying thread of hope. The words held more meaning to her than anyone would realize.

As Kimber poured her heart into the lyrics, her gaze inevitably met Rory's. At that moment, the song's narrative of a woman pleading for one more day with her husband transformed into Kimber's silent appeal to Rory. Each word was laden with her wish for another chance, a plea for just one more day to show the depth of her feelings for him. She couldn't be sure if Rory interpreted the song's message as it was intended for him, but in her heart, she hoped he understood.

When the song concluded, the surrounding guests offered their applause and, as they slowly dispersed, offered their condolences to Sophie and Chloe.

"You okay?" Avery asked, her concern clear as she rested her head against Kimber's shoulder.

Shaking her head, Kimber finally voiced her inner turmoil.

"I'm done being Stormer Heart, Avery. I'm tired… I miss my brother, and I miss this place. When he comes home, I want to be here, not off on tour. I hate the music that made Stormer. I know that's hypocritical, but it's true. The longer I'm her, the less I'm Kimber."

Avery, empathetic, looked into Kimber's eyes. "It's because of him, isn't it?" she asked gently. "And I don't mean that as a bad thing. The truth is, I was thinking about leaving, too. Now that I'm pregnant, I don't want to be on the road. Henley wants to settle down, but we won't leave you, Kimber. If you decide to stay on, we will too, but I won't travel as much."

"Well," Kimber sighed, a mix of relief and resignation in her voice. "If you're wanting to leave, that just confirms my idea that it's time to break up the band. Guess I have some calls to make tomorrow."

Avery nudged Kimber gently. "In the meantime," she said, guiding Kimber toward Rory, who was waiting by the car door. "I think you two need to talk."

As Kimber approached Rory, the weight of the day, the funeral, and her decision about Stormer Heart hung heavy on her. Yet there was a glimmer of hope, a chance for honesty, and perhaps a chance for them. The walk toward Rory felt like a journey toward a crossroads, a pivotal moment where the possibility of a new beginning, free from the confines of her celebrity persona, awaited her. The conversation that was about to unfold held the potential to change the course of both their lives, offering a chance for Kimber to be true to herself and to confront her feelings for Rory head-on.

"Avery," Rory acknowledged with a nod as she made her way past them toward her vehicle. He watched her settle into the SUV parked behind them, his expression unreadable. His attention then shifted back to Kimber, his eyes meeting hers with a complexity of emotions.

"Miss Storm," he said, maintaining a formal tone as he opened the car door for her.

Kimber paused at the threshold, a myriad of emotions swirling in her eyes.

"Rory," she began, her voice carrying a mix of regret and intensity. "I know you don't want to hear this, but I didn't lie to you in the way you think. Stormer Heart isn't me—not the real me. The person I become on stage is just pretending, a creation of my label to sell records. I don't like who I am under the makeup, never did, but I was young, naive. Stormer Heart has cost me a lot. And I can tell she's not done taking things from me. I'm sorry… really."

With those words, Kimber ducked into the SUV, her hand gently pulling the door from Rory's grasp. She settled into the seat, her gaze lingering on him as he walked around to the driver's side and got in. The ride home was enveloped in silence, a heavy, tangible silence that spoke volumes. The distance between them felt wider than ever, a chasm of unspoken words and unresolved emotions. Kimber's heart ached with the realization that her confession, her vulnerability, might not have been enough to bridge the gap between them. Rory's lack of response was a clear message to Kimber, one that pierced her heart.

He didn't *love* her back.

CHAPTER
SEVENTEEN

Rory's internal turmoil was palpable as he paced the conference room of LTI Security. His boss, Atlas, watched him with a mix of concern and frustration, his expression mirroring the seriousness of the situation.

Rory's admission, "I fucked up," hung in the air, heavy with regret.

"Yeah… you did." Atlas's response was blunt. "You shattered that woman's heart when she laid it out there for you. Do you love her, Rory?"

The question forced Rory to confront his feelings head-on. He had been wrestling with this exact question for the last three days, ever since the funeral. He had handed over the protection detail to Creed, finding it too painful to be near Kimber yet remain distant. Creed had later informed him about Kimber's heated confrontation with her manager over leaving the band, revealing the depth of her commitment to changing her life.

According to Creed, Kimber and her bandmates agreed about disbanding Stormer Heart and the Tempest, each wanting a life beyond the band. However, the manager and the label were not on the same page, insisting on one last show before releasing Kimber from her contract.

Atlas, ever observant, broke into Rory's thoughts.

"I can see you're at war with yourself, Rory. If she walks away, are you going to regret not taking a chance on her?" Atlas stood and scratched his dog, Zeus's, head. Atlas had been bringing the dog to work more and more, making Rory grin at his K-9 partner.

"Yeah, probably." Rory exhaled deeply, a hint of resignation in his voice.

Atlas then urged him to reconcile with Kimber, assuring him that she was not like the woman who had hurt his sister, Roslyn. Rory was taken aback to learn that Atlas knew about his sister's ordeal.

"Yeah, I know all about her, Rory. I make it my business to know my team's history. If there is something that can come back to bite me in the ass, I gotta be prepared."

Rory started toward the door. "I need to take care of something."

"Thattaboy," Atlas called out. "Let me know if you need anything."

Rory's heart raced as he sped out of the LTI building, his mind a whirlwind of thoughts and emotions. The drive to Kimber's house felt like the longest of his life, each mile stretching on as he mulled over the possibilities of what lay ahead. His thoughts were consumed with questions about their future and whether Kimber would forgive his recent behavior, which he now recognized as foolish and driven by fear and misunderstanding.

With a deep breath to steady his nerves, Rory stepped out of his Expedition and approached the front door. His steps were measured, each one heavy with the weight of his intentions and the uncertainty of Kimber's reception. He reached the door and knocked, the sound echoing both inside the house and in his own heightened state of awareness. He was not at all prepared for what greeted him when the door opened.

"What the fuck?" Rory growled. "Why are you dressed like that?"

"Seriously, I'm not in the mood for your shit," Kimber huffed. She turned and left him standing at the entrance.

As Rory followed Kimber into the house, he noticed Avery, Henley, and Creed gathered in the living room. Their expressions were a mix of anger and regret. It was obvious something significant had transpired. Kimber, seemingly oblivious to Avery's calls, continued her determined march upstairs.

Henley blocked Rory's path. "The record label made her do an interview—telling the fans this was going to be her last concert. She wasn't happy."

"All due respect, you need to move." Rory was trying not to lose his shit, but the woman upstairs and he had unfinished business. "I need to speak with her."

"Alright, it's your funeral." Henley sighed, understanding the gravity of the situation, yet reluctant to intervene. "Just be careful, alright?" Turning to his wife, his demeanor softened. "Avery," he said gently, "let's go grab some dinner. We need to make sure you and my unborn baby are well-fed. There's no need for us to stick around for what might turn into World War Three here."

Avery rushed to his side. "Good luck, Rory. Call me if you need me."

Rory watched as Henley and Avery made their way out of the house, leaving a palpable tension in the air. Only Creed remained, a silent observer until now. He stepped forward.

"I'll do a perimeter sweep," he said, his voice calm. "That should give you two some time to talk without interruptions."

"Thank you, Brother," he said, his voice reflecting a mix of gratitude and determination. He was ready to face whatever awaited him upstairs, knowing the conversation ahead was going to be anything but easy.

He took the steps two at a time, eager to confront Kimber. What he hadn't expected was seeing her in person as Stormer Heart. That persona embodied everything he hated—it reminded him of the issues he'd harbored since his sister's incident. Stopping outside her door, he closed his eyes and knocked.

"Kimber?" Rory called out. When he got no response, he turned the knob and stepped inside.

The bedroom felt hollow, its emptiness sending a sharp bolt of alarm through Rory. His heart pounded against his ribs, a drumbeat of rising panic. He hesitated at the threshold, about to call out Kimber's name, when the faint sound of running water from the bathroom reached his ears. A sigh of relief escaped him, muted and tense.

Stepping quietly, Rory eased his way into the room. The air was thick with the scent of her perfume, a lingering trace of her presence. He gently pushed open the bathroom door, the hinges whispering a soft protest. Rory paused, taking a moment to observe her. Kimber had shed the platinum wig, revealing her natural hair, the opposite look to the artificial glimmer of Stormer Heart. She was scrubbing her face fiercely, a desperate attempt to erase the remnants of her stage makeup. It wasn't until he noticed the reddened patches on her skin, where she had scrubbed a little too harshly, that Rory jumped into action.

"Whoa, Kimber," he said, his voice laced with worry as he gently grabbed her hands to stop her. "You're hurting yourself."

Kimber's head jerked up, her eyes meeting his. Rory inhaled sharply, taken aback by the raw emotion he saw there. Tears brimmed in her eyes, threatening to spill over. Her makeup, once meticulously applied, now streaked across her skin in chaotic trails, a stark contrast to the usual polished appearance of the pop icon. Kimber's sobs came in quiet hiccups, each one making her body tremble. The vulnerability on display was heart-wrenching.

"I hate this," Kimber whispered, her voice barely audible. "Stormer Heart has simultaneously given me everything and taken it away." Her eyes, shimmering with unshed tears, reflected a profound sense of loss.

Rory reached out, his movements tender and cautious as he stepped between her legs, pinning her against the sink. Cupping her cheek, he traced a path through the ruined makeup with his thumb.

"What do you mean, Kimber? What has she taken?"

"Everything," she whispered back, her voice cracking under the weight of her emotions.

"It hasn't, Kimber… not unless you let it." He took her chin in his hand, his grip firm but not unkind, lifting her face to meet his eyes. His gaze was intense, burning with a mix of frustration and desire. "I know you think it has, but you're wrong. It hasn't taken—"

His words were abruptly cut short, severed by the sudden intrusion of another voice, deep and unmistakably familiar.

"Kimber." The sound of Jaxson's voice rolled through the house like distant thunder, bursting the bubble they'd been in.

Rory's expression transformed from one of intense focus to surprise, a hint of annoyance flickering in his eye at the disruption. The unexpected intrusion shattered the fragile bubble of their intimate moment.

"What the fuck?" The words tumbled out of Jaxson's mouth, rough and edged with shock, as he stood at the door, taking in the scene before him. Rory was standing between her legs with his hands gently cupping her cheeks, a position that spoke volumes of their closeness. "Care to tell me why you're practically dry-humping my sister against the sink?" Jaxson's tone was accusatory, his brows furrowed in a mix of confusion and protective anger.

"Jaxson." Kimber's voice quivered with the emotions she could no longer contain as she extricated herself from Rory's hold. She practically lunged into her brother's arms, seeking solace in his familiar presence. "You're here… You're really here." Her sobs were heart-wrenching, each one echoing in the small bathroom and splintering Rory's heart further.

"I'll leave you two to talk," Rory announced. As he passed by Jaxson, he was met with a low, menacing growl of a warning.

"I love you like a brother… but we're going to talk about this, Rory. I trusted you to protect her, not… whatever that was."

Jaxson's words were laced with a sense of betrayal and disappointment.

Rory dipped his chin and slipped out of the bedroom, leaving his best friend and his heart behind. He wasn't needed there. Not with Jaxson at home to protect her. But as he reached for the door handle, Kimber's voice stopped him in his tracks.

"Rory… wait." He turned, his eyes traveling up the stairs to where Kimber was hurrying down toward him. Kimber stepped closer, her eyes searching his. "You're leaving?" The question hung between them, loaded with emotion and unspoken hopes.

Jaxson stood behind her, his presence like a shadow, his arms folded across his chest in a silent but clear message of 'don't you dare.' Rory exhaled a heavy breath and shrugged.

"I think it's for the best," he muttered, his voice tinged with resignation.

"So, it's over then?" Her voice cracked with disbelief.

"I think it has to be," he whispered, his voice barely more than a whisper as his chest tightened with pain.

Kimber's eyes blazed with a fire that Rory had never seen before as she stepped closer to him, her voice shaking with potent anger.

"You're a coward, Rory," she spat out, the words like daggers aimed straight at his heart. "If you think walking away is the easy way out, then you never really cared about me."

Jaxson grunted with shock, but Kimber kept talking. Her chest heaved with each word.

"I'll be just fine without you, believe me. If I'm not worth fighting for in your eyes, then I don't want you here. I don't need someone who gives up at the first sign of trouble. But know that you're walking away from something real, something worth every bit of the struggle."

He watched as she turned on her heel and stormed up the stairs. Her brother watched her go and didn't turn around until the master bedroom door slammed. His eyes narrowed on Rory as he took a step forward.

"I think you and I need to have a chat, *brother*."

CHAPTER
EIGHTEEN

KIMBER WANTED TO SCREAM, to let out all the frustration and anxiety that was bubbling up inside her. Everything in her life seemed to spiral out of control, leaving her feeling helpless. First, the flowers that she'd intercepted that morning were a chilling reminder that her stalker, who had been haunting her for months, was not only still watching her but was becoming more brazen in their approach. Especially since she was headed back to Nashville to end her ten-year career.

Kimber had worried that she might regret leaving the only profession she had ever known, the one thing in her life that had always been a constant, but the note that had come with the flowers that morning only confirmed that it was time to call it quits. It was time to leave behind the life she knew, to step into the unknown in search of a new journey, a new chapter where she could find peace and a sense of security that had eluded her for years.

Henley watched with a mix of concern and resignation as Kimber hurriedly packed her belongings.

"I'll support you no matter what you decide, Kimber, but maybe we should ask them to accompany us to Nashville. I'm worried about what your stalker might do when he learns you're back in town."

Kimber, absorbed in her task, hardly looked up. "What's it matter? He knows I'm here. The notes prove that."

"No." Henley's scoff cut through the air, a sound of frustration at the situation and perhaps at Kimber's dismissive attitude. "They prove he or she knew where you went."

Kimber zipped up her case with a finality that signaled the end of the argument.

"Jaxson is home, so I'm not needed here for the remodel. I need to deal with the label and tie up loose ends with the band." Her voice was firm, a clear sign her mind was made up.

Reaching forward, Henley grabbed her bag. "Fine, but at least tell your brother the *real* reason you're running out of her with your ass on fire."

"I don't know what you're talking about, Henley." Kimber's response was instantaneous, her body language shifting as she planted her hands on her hips and fixed Henley with a glare.

Henley met her gaze, his expression softening as he sighed, a sound that seemed to carry the weight of unspoken truths. "Really… you're doing exactly what I was doing—pushing him away. I can guarantee he's stepping aside because he thinks it's what you want."

"Whatever." It was a dismissal, but beneath it lay a turmoil of emotions and unacknowledged truths. Henley's words had struck a chord, a reminder of the intricate dance of relationships and the fine line between protecting oneself and pushing away those who cared. She nodded toward the door. "Lead the way."

Henley, his expression a mixture of concern and resignation, shook his head slightly as he stepped out of Kimber's room into the hallway. The air was thick with unspoken words and the tension of the moment. Kimber was determined, her mind set on fleeing the turmoil that had engulfed her life. But even as she made her final preparations, a part of her wanted to reconsider and face her problems head-on rather than run away.

As she descended the stairs, her steps quick but hesitant, her eyes immediately sought her brother. She found Jaxson exactly where she expected him to be, standing like a sentinel at the window, his gaze lost in the afternoon sky. The sight of him, so deep in thought, momentarily paused her anxious energy. Jaxson, always the steady force in her life, now seemed distant, as if he, too, was struggling with his own storms.

Jaxson, sensing her presence, turned his head slightly to look at her. His expression was unreadable, a mix of curiosity and concern.

"Leaving already, Songbird?" he asked, his voice calm but carrying an undertow of emotion. It was a simple question, but laden with the weight of everything that remained unsaid between them.

As she stood there, facing Jaxson, she realized this might be her last chance to open up, to share her fears and hopes, and to seek the support and understanding she so desperately needed. But how did she explain to him that she was in love with his best friend, a man who had rejected her? She didn't want to cause tension, rather more tension, between them. Kimber knew she was the reason Jaxson hadn't talked to Rory since he found them in the bathroom together.

Kimber walked toward him and stopped inches from where he stood. Her eyes, mirrors of her determination and vulnerability, locked onto his. "

"It's only temporary," she declared. "I'll be back before you know it, and you'll be wishing for privacy again."

He looked down at her, the corners of his mouth lifting in a gentle, knowing smile. "Not true, songbird," he replied, his voice low. The affectionate nickname, a nod to her musical talent, and the way her voice had always seemed to reach directly into his soul hung between them.

Kimber wrapped her arms tightly around Jaxson's middle, her embrace a testament to the years of distance and missed moments. Pressing her cheek against the solid strength of his frame, she felt a wave of security wash over her, a feeling only a brother's presence could provide. She inhaled deeply. The familiar scent of Jaxson, a blend of the aftershave he'd used since they were teenagers and a hint of sunshine, filled her senses. God, how she'd missed this—the comfort, the safety. Their lives—hers, a whirlwind of touring and his marked by military deployments—had kept their worlds apart, tethered only by fleeting calls and sporadic visits.

Kimber's thoughts drifted back to her childhood and teenage years, a time when Jaxson's towering presence was a constant. His shadow had been her sanctuary, her playground, a place where she felt invincible. Now, standing here, engulfed in his embrace, a pang of melancholy hit her.

"I missed you," she mumbled into the fabric of his shirt, her voice a mix of longing and relief. "You're coming to Nashville, right?" she asked, a hint of hope lacing her words.

Jaxson's expression shifted, his brows knitting together in a mix of concern. "I'm most definitely coming, Kimber," he said firmly. "You have a fucking stalker, and I'm not leaving you alone until we sort this out." He paused, his voice hardening. "His last note was creepy as fuck."

Kimber's body stiffened at his words, a shiver of fear echoing through her body. Jaxson didn't know the extent of it. The latest note, the one she had crumpled up in a fit of denial and shoved into the bottom of her suitcase, was far worse. If he saw it, she knew it would send him spiraling into a vortex of rage. She was acutely aware she was ignoring a potential threat, a dangerous game, but the chaos of the past months had left her craving normalcy, even if it was a façade. She wanted—no, needed—to pretend, if only for a moment, that this ominous cloud wasn't hovering over her life.

Suppressing the gnawing truth clawing at her insides, Kimber took a deliberate step back, creating a physical distance that mirrored her internal struggle.

"Henley will make sure I'm safe," she asserted, her voice steady despite the way she was feeling. "Besides, this person hasn't really done anything. Just a bunch of empty threats, that's all." The words felt hollow even as they left her lips, her stomach twisting into knots of worry.

Jaxson's gaze bore into her. "You know escalation is the next step, Kim. I can't stand the thought of you getting hurt."

Kimber moved toward the door, her steps hesitant. She paused, her back to him.

"This is it, the last concert. After this weekend, Stormer Heart is history. Maybe then, this stalker will just forget about me."

"What if they don't?" Jaxson challenged, his arms crossed firmly over his chest in frustration. "What if they decide to make their move now? I get that this is important to you, Kimber, but your life… it's worth more than any show."

She turned. "Tell that to my manager and the label. I've poured a decade into this, Jax. If I back out now, they'll strip me of everything. I can't let that happen. Henley and his team are on it. I trust them."

"If you truly believed that, you wouldn't have come home." Jaxson's retort was swift, laced with a mix of anger and fear.

Kimber's response was a soft shake of her head, a gesture of resignation. "I have to do this. Please, Jax, don't add to my burden. I promise to be careful. To ease your mind, I'll even have Henley consult with LTI for extra security."

Jaxson's eyes narrowed, understanding the gravity of her compromise. Kimber hadn't even mentioned Rory in days, and suggesting LTI, a firm he worked with, was a big step for her, a sign of her own underlying fears.

"Fine," Kimber acquiesced, her voice tinged with irritation. "I'll be a good girl and stick to Henley like glue." Her words carried a hint of sarcasm as she stepped out onto the porch, the wooden boards creaking under her feet.

Jaxson's concern followed her like a shadow. He stepped out after her, planting himself firmly at the top of the steps, his posture rigid with the weight of his protective instincts.

"Seriously, Kimber," he called out as she reached for her car door. His eyes were earnest, pleading. "Henley," he shouted, directing his gaze toward his trusted friend, who had been waiting for Kimber to leave. The plan was for Henley to follow Kimber all the way to their shared compound, ensuring nothing went wrong between Alabama and Nashville. "You better make sure she's safe until I get there."

"Don't worry, Jaxson, I got her," Henley's voice carried a reassuring solidity, a promise in the form of words.

"Love you, big brother," Kimber called out, her voice softening. She blew him a kiss as she slid behind the wheel of her car—one that sported a new paint coat, visually erasing the whole reason she'd come to Alabama to begin with.

As she started the engine and began to drive away, Kimber glanced in the rearview mirror. The image of her brother, standing resolutely on the porch, grew smaller with each passing moment. A poignant sensation welled up inside her, a mix of love, gratitude, and an unnamable ache. It wasn't just the physical distance from Jaxson that tugged at her heartstrings. Her thoughts inevitably drifted to a certain six-foot-four man who had accidentally claimed a piece of her heart. Despite their parting and the tension that lingered between them, she couldn't shake his image from her mind. He had burrowed deep into her heart, leaving a lifelong mark on her soul.

As the road stretched out before her, Kimber's mind wrestled with doubts and hopes. She clung to the belief that her decision was the right one, that the sacrifices and risks she was taking were necessary. Because if they weren't, if she had misjudged the situation, then everything she was doing, every step she was taking, was in vain.

And that was a thought too scary to fully embrace.

CHAPTER
NINETEEN

THE CONFERENCE ROOM buzzed with tense energy, the air thick with anticipation and unease as the team awaited the fire investigator's arrival. Ares had even appeared for the meeting, which shocked Rory. He hadn't seen Ares in years—he, too, was a former Navy SEAL. All three Lyons brothers had made a career out of the Navy.

Rory sat there, his anxiety palpable, not just from the impending meeting, but from the weight of everything else on his mind. It was Friday, and the clock was ticking down to Kimber's farewell concert on Saturday night—a fact Jaxson, after a heated confrontation that had left Rory with a bruised jaw, made abundantly clear. Jaxson still hadn't forgiven Rory, and he suspected it would take a while—especially since, according to him, Rory had broken Kimber's heart.

The weight of his realization settled heavily in Rory's chest, a gnawing discomfort that twisted into a knot of nausea. The thought that he had contributed to Kimber's heartache was more than just a passing concern—it was a visceral, gut-wrenching acknowledgment. It wasn't just her heart that bore the scars of their complicated dance; his own heart felt like it had been shredded, as if it had been fed through a relentless meat grinder of regret.

Each pulse in his veins was a reminder of the love he tried to bury, the emotions he attempted to dismiss. But love, he realized, wasn't something that could be switched off at will. It clung to the crevices of his heart, stubborn and unyielding. The more he tried to distance himself from his feelings for Kimber, the more entangled he became in the web of his own affections. Rory grappled with the magnitude of his emotions. The realization that he had inflicted pain on both Kimber, and himself, was a bitter pill to swallow.

"Are you even listening?" Atlas's voice cut through Rory's thoughts. His boss' irritation was clear as he tossed a pen at Rory's head, a sign that his distraction was unacceptable. "Rory, I get that you're distracted, but this is crucial."

Jaxson, who had been observing Rory with a blend of frustration and concern, leaned forward abruptly. He tossed an item onto the table, capturing everyone's attention.

"My sister thinks she's being clever, but she missed something when she was packing."

Rory's hand shot out, snatching the crumpled note from the table. The words scrawled on it sent a chill down his spine.

Your last concert will be a farewell no one will forget. Lights, sound… bang. A fitting ending for a bitch and a phony. Everyone will remember you… and the truth will set me free. Enjoy your last few nights alive because soon, your last breath will be mine.

"What the fuck?" Rory muttered, passing the ominous note to Davis, who was seated beside him. "She didn't mention this to you?"

"Nope," Jaxson replied, the word popping sharply. "She's been too preoccupied with the show and… other things." His pointed glare at Rory left no doubt about what he meant. "I've spoken with Henley. He assured me she hasn't left the compound, and there haven't been any more suspicious deliveries."

"We need to coordinate with the investigator and devise a strategy," Atlas interjected. "Henley's already requested extra security for the concert night. He's got three of his own staff, plus the venue security on board."

Creed, who had been quietly listening, chimed in from his corner of the room. "And we all know how reliable venue staff can be… mostly young college kids looking for a quick buck."

The conversation was halted abruptly by a gentle tap at the door. Hilda, a family friend and now the office secretary, peered in with an apologetic smile. "Sorry to interrupt, boys, but the investigator from Birmingham is here," she announced in her familiar, warm tone, her presence a comforting constant in the often-chaotic office environment.

A well-put-together man stepped into the room. Ares Lyons, the leader of their team, rose to his feet and extended a hand in greeting.

"Hello, thank you for coming by," he said with a firm handshake. "I'm Ares Lyons. Let me introduce you to the team." As Ares introduced each member seated around the table, there was a palpable sense of anxiety. When he reached Jaxson, Ares gestured toward him. "And this is Jaxson Storm. His house is the one in question."

The investigator introduced himself as Noah Ripley from the Birmingham Fire Investigators Office. He acknowledged each team member with a nod before addressing Jaxson.

"Nice to meet you, Mr. Storm," he said in a tone that balanced professionalism with empathy. "I'm Investigator Noah Ripley. Chief Phillips sent me after the firefighters reported finding some unusual evidence."

Rory, who had been following the conversation intently, leaned forward, his interest piqued. "Interesting? What do you mean? We thought it was due to old pipes or something along those lines."

Investigator Ripley delved into the findings of their investigation. He presented several photos and detailed accounts that painted a disturbing picture. It became clear that the situation was far more sinister than a mere accident. The gas line hadn't simply corroded over time as they had initially thought; it had been deliberately cut. This revelation sent a wave of shock and concern through the room, as the implications of such an act meant that the notes to Kimber were more than simple threats.

"Fuck," Jaxson muttered under his breath, his frustration palpable as Ripley exited the room. He stood up abruptly, a man propelled by a sense of urgency. "I need to get Henley on the phone. Kimber's in more danger than she realizes."

Ares, who had been observing the unfolding events with a strategic eye, leaned back in his chair. His gaze was sharp and calculating as he asked, "Any idea who could be behind this?"

"None." Jaxson gave a helpless shrug, his frustration evident. "And even if Kimber had the slightest clue, I doubt she'd tell me. She's always been tight-lipped about her personal life."

At this point, Atlas, who had been allowing Ares to take the lead, chimed in. His voice was calm. "Davis," he said, addressing one of the team members. "I need you to look into Kimber's life." Turning to Jaxson, he raised his hand preemptively. "And Jaxson," he continued, "before you get defensive, understand that this is necessary. We need to identify anyone from the past few years who might hold a grudge or have a motive."

Rory watched as a myriad of emotions flickered across Jaxson's face. He understood his friend's reluctance to pry into Kimber's private life. However, given the severity of the situation, with

Kimber's safety at stake, they needed to dig deeper. Kimber hadn't been forthcoming about the extent of the threats she faced. If they were to protect her effectively, they had no choice but to peel back the layers of her life and uncover whatever secrets she had been keeping hidden. It was a necessary, though uncomfortable, intrusion for the sake of her keeping her alive, seeing as one attempt had already been made.

"Rory, you and Jaxson head to Nashville tonight," Atlas directed, his tone brooking no argument. "We'll keep your presence there low-key for the time being. If Kimber gets wind of the real reason you're there, she might react impulsively, and we can't afford any reckless moves on her part. Davis will start the background work."

Davis, who had been listening intently, flashed a wry smile as he stood up. "Nothing like hitting the ground running," he remarked with a mix of humor and determination. He glanced at Jaxson, his expression turning serious. "Don't worry, we've got you and your sister's back." Then, turning to Rory, his smile returned with an edge of camaraderie. "And you," he said, clapping a hand on Rory's shoulder. "You need to pull your head out of your ass and go save your girl." The words, though lightly spoken, carried the weight of a man who shared an unspoken understanding of Rory's situation.

The room gradually emptied, leaving Rory and Jaxson alone in the silent aftermath of the meeting. Rory turned toward Jaxson, his expression filled with honest regret.

"You're like a brother to me, Jaxson. I'm sorry I wasn't upfront about everything, but I won't apologize for my feelings. Falling for Kimber… it wasn't something I planned."

"Fall for her?" Jaxson's response was filled with skepticism and underlined with frustration. "Then why the hell did you let her go, Rory?" He scoffed, disbelief etching his features. "And don't tell me it's because of me. If that was your reason, you never really loved her."

Rory's reaction was swift, his emotions boiling over as he stepped up to Jaxson, their faces inches apart.

"Don't you dare question my feelings," he retorted, his voice laced with passion. "She deserves someone better than me. You know my issues with people from her world. You know what happened with my sister, Roslyn. So does Kimber. I never want her to feel like I question her because of the status of her bank account."

"You hear yourself?" Jaxson pushed him back, his own emotions flaring. "You're basically saying she's like those who hurt Roslyn. When will you let go of the past and see that there are good people like my sister? Kimber isn't the person you think she is. Stormer Heart is just a persona, Rory. That's not who she really is.

"I'll meet you back here in an hour," he had said, his voice filled with bitterness and laced with urgency as he brushed past Rory, his figure momentarily framed in the doorway before vanishing.

Jaxson's departure left a palpable silence in the room, a void filled only by the echo of his parting words.

Rory stood there, alone, the emptiness of the room amplifying the turbulent surge of his thoughts. Each second that ticked by in Jaxson's absence was a stark reminder of the conversation that had just unfolded, the words lingering in the air like fragments of a storm. He replayed the exchange in his mind, each sentence punctuated by the weight of truth and the heaviness of unspoken emotions.

"Fuck," he muttered to himself, a newfound resolve swirling within him. He understood, with a clarity that was almost painful, that the time for doubts and hesitations had passed. Rory was done with pushing Kimber away, done with allowing the ghosts of his past to dictate his future. The realization that she was his, a truth he had fought against, now seemed as undeniable as the beating of his heart.

Rory's resolve was no longer just about protecting Kimber from the immediate threat—it was about reclaiming the love he had almost let slide through his fingers. It was about facing his fears, tearing down the walls he had built around his heart, and embracing the vulnerability that came with love. He was ready to win back the heart of the woman who had unwittingly claimed his own.

It was time to go slay some monsters.

CHAPTER
TWENTY

NOTHING, absolutely nothing, was swinging in Kimber's favor that day. The very essence of the evening seemed to conspire against her, starting with the costume debacle. The outfit selected for her by her stylist, usually so in tune with her tastes, now appeared as if it were the cruelest joke ever played. It was, without a doubt, the most hideous ensemble she had ever laid eyes on. The members of her band, Stormer Heart and the Tempests, shared in her dismay, equally disgruntled about their own clothing disasters.

Kimber couldn't help but wonder if this was some twisted method of the label sending a clear, unspoken message... a resounding 'fuck you.' Yet, amidst this fashion disaster, there was one solitary element that Kimber admired—her sleek, black patent leather knee-high stiletto boots, a small beacon of style in a sea of clothing chaos. She reached up, adjusting the wig that now felt like a leaden chain around her neck, an uncomfortable reminder of the façade she was forced to uphold.

The thick layer of makeup plastered on her skin was another source of discomfort. It felt like a mask, making Kimber want to claw at her own face just to feel some semblance of the real her.

She stood there, a physical manifestation of everything she wasn't, each element of her appearance a betrayal of her authentic self. The woman reflected in the mirror was a stranger, an elaborate construct designed to please and entertain, but in doing so, she had lost sight of who she truly was. Kimber felt a deep sense of revulsion, not just at the front she presented to the world, but at the thought of Rory seeing her in this guise—this distorted, exaggerated version of herself.

She knew all too well what he thought of the industry's artificiality, the way it molded and shaped individuals into unrecognizable versions of themselves. And here she was, the personification of that artificiality, representing everything he despised. It was a bitter pill to swallow, realizing she had become the exact image of the superficiality he despised. She could almost hear his voice in her head, his words laced with disdain for the industry's penchant for façade over genuineness.

She *hated* it with every fiber of her being.

Casting a glance around the room, Kimber observed her bandmates. A recent revelation had left her in a state of shock—they, too, were utterly burned out and embraced the same desire to dissolve Stormer Heart and the Tempests. This was a development Kimber never saw coming—her bandmates longing to escape the very stage they once craved. Their reasons for wanting to step out of the limelight weren't aligned with hers, a detail she regretted not sharing with them earlier. However, Henley, her head of security, believed in keeping the circle of those aware of her stalker situation as small as possible.

"I'm glad you did this, Kimber. I've been afraid to mention it to you guys." Charlie, aka Pixie, their drummer, shrugged her shoulders as she plopped down on the chair near the window. "Honestly, this life is becoming exhausting, and I have enough money that I can do something else. I've been smart with my investments."

Roxy, their electric guitarist, feigned shock. "You mean you're not on the brink of bankruptcy?"

"Not even close," Charlie replied with a smug grin. "The challenge now is figuring out what's next. I entered this industry for the love of music, not for the endless rigmarole and pretense it's become."

They exchanged stories of what ifs and possibilities about what they'd been thinking about for when they each left Nashville. Roxie wanted to record some music she'd been working on that was the complete opposite of the stuff they'd been playing for the last ten years. Charlie wanted to travel for a while, see the world as a bystander. She was tired of the constant hotels and secrecy. They weren't able to explore the places they'd visited for fear we'd be outed as Stormer Heart and the Tempests. Star talked about visiting her family and seeing her nieces and nephews. She felt guilty about missing them growing up.

"I, for one, am ready to start a family," Madison, aka Electra, the keyboardist, interrupted. "Mikey and I want kids. All this constant traveling around isn't going to work forever."

"Wow, guys. Why didn't you say something sooner?" Kimber looked at her longtime friends, absorbing their sentiments and reflecting on her own journey. "When I moved to Nashville, I saw being true to myself, not hiding behind layers of makeup and losing my identity. This isn't the dream I chased."

"Perhaps this is the right move." Star, the band's electric violinist, added her thoughts. "I treasure our bond, and I don't want to lose that, but we all seem to crave a change, and I'm just as weary as the rest of you."

Charlie looked up at Kimber, a hint of curiosity in her eyes. "What about you, Kimber? What's your next move? You're not planning to linger around here, are you?"

"Home," Kimber sighed, her thoughts turning homeward. "I miss my brother, and I think Avery wants to go back as well. One of my old friends is going to need some help—her husband was killed in an accident while I was there visiting. She and her daughter don't have many people. I want to be there for her."

"What about the hunky guy you told us about?" Madison waggled her eyebrows. "Surely, you're going to get more of that."

A smile flickered across Kimber's face, her mind drifting to the man who hadn't shown up yet at the venue. It frustrated her to see everyone from Lyons Tactical except him. When she had inquired about his absence, her brother had simply shrugged, stating he was following new leads and would arrive before their performance. Despite considering him completely off-limits, a tiny, hopeful part of her clung to the possibility that maybe, just maybe, he hadn't intended to push her away so definitely.

"It was just a fleeting moment. He despises our kind of people and made it quite clear that there's no chance for anything between us," Kimber said, trying to sound convincing.

"Bullshit," Avery announced, bursting into the room. "That man is like a caged animal out there."

Kimber's heart skipped a beat. "He's here?"

Avery rolled her eyes dramatically. "Yes, Kimber, he's here. And he's causing a scene, demanding you cancel the show. Rory and Jaxson nearly got into a fight with Bryce over it. He's furious."

Perplexed, Kimber asked, "But why? Why cancel the concert?"

At that moment, the door flew open, and Hensley burst in, pulling Avery close.

"Because, Kimber," he said with a grave tone, "someone is trying to kill you."

The room was a whirlwind of emotion, a gale of concern, anger, and confusion swirling around Kimber. Her bandmates, unsurprisingly, were incensed, not just about the ominous notes Kimber had received but also about her decision to take a break without fully disclosing the reason. Their frustration was palpable, tinged with a genuine worry that Kimber was underestimating the gravity of her situation. But her perspective was different. To her, surrendering to the stalker's intimidation by canceling her show would be equivalent to conceding defeat. She was weary of being commanded by unseen forces, be it the stalker or the label itself. This concert, possibly her last, was her stand against being controlled. Defiantly, Kimber stood up, her movements signaling a turning point.

"You know what?" she declared, a fierce determination in her voice as she ripped off her wig. "I'm done being told what to do. I'm not wearing this fucking wig or this clown makeup for one more minute. I'm finished with it all."

"Whoa, Kimber, what are you doing?" Avery, concerned and slightly alarmed, followed Kimber into the adjoining small bathroom. "You can't just go out there without your costume."

"I can, and I will," Kimber responded, her voice resolute. "I'm done living up to their expectations. Tonight, I'm singing something from my heart." She quickly and thoroughly scrubbed her face clean, erasing the layers of makeup.

"Hey, guys," Kimber called out to her band, her voice echoing with newfound excitement and determination. "I want to play something tonight. Are you with me?" She rummaged through her bag and pulled out a journal containing a song she had penned, a piece of her soul in lyrical form.

As the journal made its rounds among her bandmates, their expressions transformed from concern to smiles of agreement and admiration.

"I love this," Charlie beamed, her eyes reflecting the joy of the moment. "I think it's doable. Guys?" The others nodded in agreement, solidifying Kimber's decision.

"It's settled then," Kimber declared, turning to Avery and Hensley with a look of unwavering resolve. "You two need to keep the label out of our hair. We're going to use the next little while to rehearse this. It might be a total fiasco, but I don't care. It's high time the world saw the real Kimber Storm and her band."

They were up against the clock, with only forty minutes until showtime. These precious minutes would be spent crafting their rebellion, a bold statement against the label's constraints.

Avery, though hesitant, eventually nodded in agreement. "Fine, but Hensley and I need to talk to Jaxson and Atlas to figure out the full story behind Rory's outburst. In the meantime, lock the door and stay safe. Creed's standing guard outside."

With the plan set, the room transformed into a hub of creative energy, each member contributing to the new direction. This was not just a performance—it was a declaration of independence, a farewell to the shackles of expectation, and a daring leap into authenticity. For Kimber and her band, it was the culmination of their journey, a moment where they could finally show the world who they truly were on their terms.

They could either exit the stage with a resonant, high note, a performance that would leave their fans with a lingering hunger for the genuine, unadulterated essence of their true selves.

Or her choice to unveil her true self to the world might lead to irreversible consequences.

Either way, Kimber's heart knew that while she was on the right path, her journey was not yet complete, and the lingering 'almost' was a reminder that there were still chapters to be written, stories to be told, and resolutions to be found.

CHAPTER
TWENTY-ONE

RORY'S EMOTIONS were a raging storm, a mix of anger and apprehension churning within him as the pieces of the puzzle began to fall into place. The revelation that Kimber's stalker was acquainted with her, someone who knew the nuances of her life and her past, was deeply unsettling. It suggested a betrayal of trust, a violation that was both personal and sinister. The fact that this individual held a grudge only amplified the threat.

"I don't get it," he muttered, his voice a mix of confusion and frustration. Jaxson was pacing back and forth like a caged animal. "Everyone loves Kimber… there hasn't been a single person—" He stopped mid-sentence and suddenly froze, a look of dawning realization washing over his face. "Oh, fuck," he exclaimed, the pieces of the puzzle clicking into place in his mind.

Rory, sensing the gravity of Jaxson's epiphany, fixed his gaze on him. "What is it?" he demanded. "You think you know who's behind this?"

Jaxson shook his head, his features etched with disbelief. "Before Henley took over, Kimber's head of security was this guy, Jon Maybury. He'd been the labels go-to guy for security for years." Jaxson's voice was heavy with regret. "When he first started working for Kimber, she complained about him being overly attentive, almost smothering. I thought she was just being young and dramatic, but over time, his behavior grew increasingly controlling."

Rory interjected, seeking clarity. "You mean protective?"

"No," Jaxson corrected, his tone firm. "Possessive. He'd get irrationally angry when Kimber and the band tried to have a normal night out. It was beyond professional concern." Jaxson's fingers flew over his phone as he dialed Davis, needing more information about Maybury.

As Rory paced, his mind raced with concern as Jaxson spoke in hushed, urgent tones to Davis. Rory, not wanting to waste a moment, called Henley into the room to join the discussion.

Henley entered, his expression questioning. "What's going on? You guys have a lead?"

Rory nodded gravely. "Jaxson thinks it's Maybury, the guy you replaced."

"Maybury? I wouldn't put it past him." Henley's response was immediate, a mixture of realization and anger. "He was bitter about being let go. Wait, there's more." Henley's mind raced as he pieced together the series of odd incidents they'd experienced. Henley began recounting all the weird things that happened over the six months. Mysterious letters, coupled with failing equipment, had Henley thinking Jaxson was right on target with his assessment.

"God damn it." Jaxson, ending his call, looked up with a grim expression. "Davis just confirmed Maybury was fired from another security job six months ago. Kimber met the singer he was guarding in Austin, and she mentioned her past issues with Jon. It's unbelievable he was still working as personal protection."

Rory's mind raced, connecting the dots. "He blames Kimber," he growled, a cold awareness setting in. "The letters, the recent attempts on her life… it all makes sense now. We can't let her go on stage tonight. Maybury might see this event as the perfect opportunity for his twisted revenge." The urgency of the situation was palpable, a race against time to protect Kimber from a threat that had just become terrifyingly real.

"She's already on stage." As Henley delivered the update, his voice was tinged with resignation. "That's exactly why I was right outside the door when you guys opened it. I was coming to get you," he explained, his sigh betraying his anxiety. "Atlas is already blending in with the crowd, and Zeus, his dog, is with him. As for the stage, Creed, Ares, and Luca, the recruit, are strategically positioned around it."

Jaxson's concern grew into outright fear. "Jesus Christ, my sister is like a sitting duck out there," he muttered, a mix of anger and worry lacing his words.

Without wasting another moment, Jaxson and Rory followed Henley out of the back room, the distant roar of the crowd growing louder as they approached the stage.

"She just went on," Avery reported, her smile a stark contrast to the tense atmosphere. "The crowd is going wild."

Henley turned to Avery, his expression serious. "Baby, I need to lock you in the sound booth," he said, his voice firm but laced with concern. Avery's initial reaction was to protest, but Henley's reassuring arm around her and a few whispered words seemed to calm her, and she nodded, agreeing to be escorted to the safer confines of the sound booth.

As Rory glanced out onto the stage, his breath caught in his throat. "Holy shit," he exclaimed, his eyes widening with awe and surprise.

Jaxson, standing beside him, chuckled lightly. "You got that right. She's giving the label the biggest 'eff you' right now."

Rory couldn't tear his gaze away from the stage. Kimber, standing tall in her three-inch stiletto boots that accentuated her legs up to mid-thigh, was a vision of pure sexiness. The leather leggings she wore clung to her like a second skin, showcasing her every curve. But what truly captivated Rory was her hair—long, wavy, and unrestrained, a stark departure from the platinum wig and heavy makeup she had been known for. There she stood, Kimber Storm, in her most genuine form.

"How y'all doing tonight?" Kimber's voice, clear and strong, echoed over the crowd. "I know you're probably shocked to see me like this, but I assure you, I am Stormer Heart... only I'm not. My name is Kimber Storm, and for ten years, I've been hidden beneath the makeup. Tonight, I want to show you the real me... the real us." She gestured toward her bandmates, who were also devoid of their usual costumes. "We're here to give you a taste of who we truly are before we say goodbye. So, how about it? Y'all still want to hear us play?"

The response from the crowd was immediate and thunderous, a chorus of cheers and chants filling the air. As the band struck up the first notes of their pop hit, Kimber lost herself in the music, her voice rising above the commotion, a blend of passion, vulnerability, and raw energy. At this moment, she was unapologetically embracing her true self in front of thousands, regardless of the outcome.

Rory's gaze swept over the teeming crowd, a sense of unease gnawing at him. Amid the sea of faces, the threat felt ominously close, like a shadow lurking just out of sight. His attention was partially on Jaxson, who was communicating through the discrete earpiece Ares had provided to the entire team.

"Rory, don't let my sister get away." Jaxson's voice crackled in his ear, a statement that momentarily pulled Rory's focus from the crowd.

Confused, Rory glanced toward Jaxson's position on the other side of the stage. "What are you talking about? She's up there, in the middle of her performance."

"I don't mean right now." Jaxson's voice was earnest, a hint of brotherly protectiveness seeping through. "I'm talking about the long run. Look, I've seen the way you look at her. You're in love with my sister. And despite my initial reaction, I think you're the right guy for her."

Rory's hand instinctively moved to rub his jaw where Jaxson's surprise had landed. His eyes drifted back to Kimber, taking in her glowing presence on the stage. At that moment, she wasn't just a performer—she was the embodiment of everything he admired and longed for.

"Alright, Nashville," Kimber's voice filled the air. "Before I say goodbye, there's one last song I want to share. This one goes out to someone incredibly special. Someone who's been on my mind, someone I hope might be mine someday."

"She's laying it all out there, man." Jaxson's voice broke into Rory's thoughts. "After this crazy night, I hope you step up and sort things out with her."

Rory was barely able to process Jaxson's words, his senses overwhelmed by the melodic cadence of Kimber's singing. Her voice seemed to weave through the air, reaching out to him and stirring emotions deep within his heart. He stood there, transfixed, the surrounding noise fading into a distant hum as he became wholly enveloped in the emotional serenade unfolding before him.

In this world of masks and shadows, where pretenses play a part,

You saw right through the layers, straight into my heart,

You didn't need a hero, just a love that's tried and true,

You loved me for me, and that's why I love you.

No need for the spotlight, no need for a show,

In your eyes, I found a place where real love would grow,

In your embrace, I've found my shining star,

You love me for who I am, just the way you are.

You love me for me, and that's what sets us free,

In the wild, wild world, you're the one who sees,

All the imperfections and scars that I bear,

You love me for me, and you're the answer to my prayer.

. . .

KIMBER'S WORDS ENVELOPED HIM, seeping into the deepest recesses of his soul. It was a profound awakening to the truth he had been tiptoeing around—he was irrevocably in love with her. It was a sentiment that had crept up on him, quietly and steadily, like the slow rise of dawn. Despite his guarded walls, his efforts to maintain a professional distance, Kimber had effortlessly breezed past his defenses, embedding herself into the very fabric of his being.

You love me for me, and that's what sets us free,

In the wild, wild world, you're the one who sees,

All the imperfections and scars that I bear,

You love me for me, and you're the answer to my prayer.

YOU LOVE ME FOR ME, you are my guiding light,

In the storms of life, you make everything right,

With you, I'm complete, no matter how near or far,

You love me for me, you're my shining star.

RORY MADE a silent vow to himself—to embrace the vulnerability, to open his heart, and to see where this unexpected journey with Kimber might lead. As her song wound down,

Ares' voice came through. His tone sent chills straight through Rory's veins.

"Target's on the move. I can't get through the crowd. Someone, get to the front of the stage, now!" The message was stark, its urgency unmistakable.

Adrenaline surging, Rory leaped from the shadows at the side of the stage, his eyes scanning the frenzied crowd. Time seemed to warp, slowing down and speeding up all at once. He spotted the gunman in the front row, weapon raised, a stark contrast to the oblivious partying around him. The crowd, lost in the concert's exciting climax, remained unaware of the unfolding danger.

In a heartbeat, two things happened simultaneously. Ares, in a desperate bid to intervene, released Zeus, his dog. A deafening blast shattered the air, resonating with a finality that chilled Rory to his core. The shooter and Kimber both crumpled to the ground.

"Kimber!" Rory's cry tore through the commotion, raw and laden with terror. He rushed to her side, dropping to his knees. His hand instinctively sought her chest, searching for signs of life. Kimber's eyes flickered open, and she gasped out his name, her voice a frail whisper carrying the weight of her pain.

"Rory," she murmured, her words barely audible over the chaos.

"No, baby, don't talk," Rory urged, his voice a mix of desperation and tenderness. He looked around wildly, the crowd beginning to scatter in panic. Jaxson was clambering back onto the stage, his expression contorted with a mix of fury and despair.

"You're going to be okay, Kimber. Just stay with me," Rory implored, intertwining his fingers with hers. His other hand pressed against her wound, trying futilely to stem the flow of blood.

Kimber's eyes, brimming with tears, locked onto Rory's.

"Rory… I'm sorry… I lied," she stammered, each word a struggle.

"Shh, baby, it's okay. We'll talk about it later," Rory soothed, his heart breaking at her confession.

"No, Rory…" Kimber's voice was a thin thread of sound, her tears cutting through him. "I won't… I should've listened. I love…" Her voice trailed off, her eyes fluttering shut, leaving her words hanging in the air, unfinished and haunting.

Rory's world crumbled around him as he held her hand, her silent, motionless form a stark, heartbreaking contrast to the vibrant, fiery woman who had just been pouring her soul out on stage. He had vowed to open his heart, but now, as he held the fading life of the woman he loved in his arms, he was confronted with the brutal fragility of it all.

CHAPTER
TWENTY-TWO

Kimber lay there, a world of pain enveloping her entire being, an all-consuming agony that seemed to pulse through her with every labored heartbeat. It was an indescribable torment, akin to being impaled with a searing, white-hot poker. Every attempt to draw breath was an ordeal. Each inhalation felt like inhaling molten flames. Her eyelids, heavy as lead and seemingly sealed shut, resisted her efforts to open them, as if bound by an invisible force.

With a herculean effort, Kimber forced her eyes open, blinking rapidly as the harsh glare of light assaulted her sensitive pupils. She squinted, trying to adjust to the brightness, a dull throb pulsating behind her eyes.

"Hey there, Songbird." The familiar, gentle voice of her brother Jaxson broke through the haze of pain, coaxing her eyes to open wider. There was a tremor of relief, mixed with deep concern, in his tone. "Damn it, Kimber. I thought I'd lost you."

His words unleashed a flood of memories, the events of the night cascading back into her consciousness.

"I was shot," she whispered, the realization dawning on her like a slow, creeping nightmare.

"Yeah, you were," Jaxson confirmed, his voice heavy with a cocktail of emotions—relief, sorrow, and a tinge of anger.

Kimber sucked in a sharp breath, the action sending a fresh wave of pain coursing through her. She winced, the sensation similar to a thousand needles piercing her chest.

"Why?" she gasped out, the word barely more than a breathless whisper.

Her mind raced, trying to piece together the fragments of the night—the excitement of the performance, the revelation of her true self, and the sudden, shattering intrusion of violence. As Kimber lay there, struggling with the physical and emotional pain of her ordeal, the search for answers seemed both necessary and vague, a puzzle that was as complex as it was critical.

Jaxson's voice was heavy with regret, a mix of sorrow and self-reproach coloring his words. "He was holding a grudge," he mumbled almost inaudibly.

Kimber, still grappling with the haze of pain and medication, looked at him in confusion. "Who?" she asked, her voice weak.

Jaxson gently took her hand, his grip tender yet filled with unspoken apologies.

"Kimber, I'm sorry I didn't listen to you about Jon all those years ago. You had a feeling that something wasn't right with him, and I just… I blew it off."

The realization dawned on Kimber slowly, an icy wave of understanding washing over her.

"Wait… are you saying Jon Maybury was the one who shot me?" she questioned, a mix of shock and disbelief in her voice. She attempted to sit up, to confront this new reality head-on.

"No, sis, don't sit up," Jaxson urged, his voice laced with concern. "You've got stitches in your chest. The bullet…" He paused, struggling to compose himself as emotion threatened to overwhelm him. "It entered on your left side. If it had been just a few inches to the right, it… it would have killed you. You're going to be sore for quite some time, and you'll probably need physical therapy for your shoulder. If Rory hadn't been there or had the quick thinking of getting Luca over to you…" His words trailed off.

Kimber's thoughts immediately flew to Rory. She closed her eyes, the memory of him holding her hand, his presence a comforting anchor in the chaos, resurfacing in her mind.

"Rory," she whispered, her voice tinged with worry and longing. "Where is he?"

At that moment, the room seemed to close in around her. Kimber closed her eyes and tried to push down the tears threatening to bubble up. The walls echoed with the unspoken fear that lingered in the air. Her question hung there, filled with a deep-seated need to see him, to reassure herself of his safety, to reconnect with the man who had been her devoted protector in her most vulnerable moment. Kimber's heart ached with a myriad of emotions for Rory that went beyond words. The intensity of the whole situation had peeled back layers of her feelings, revealing a depth of emotion she could no longer deny or ignore.

She was in love with him.

"Where's who?" Rory's deep voice cut through Kimber's trance, snapping her back to the present. Startled, her eyes flew open, not realizing until that moment that she had been so deeply lost in thought, she hadn't even heard the door to her hospital room open. Kimber blinked, as if the man standing in the doorway was a mirage. Beside her, Jaxson, who had been a silent sentinel at her bedside, gave her hand a reassuring squeeze.

"I'll leave you two to talk. And Kimber," he muttered, leaning down to plant a gentle kiss on her cheek. Before pulling away, he whispered just loud enough for her to hear, "Don't throw something good away."

Kimber met her brother's gaze with a hint of vulnerability. "I don't plan on it," she replied, her voice barely above a murmur.

"Good." Jaxson then turned toward Rory, enveloping him in a brief hug. "Take care of her, brother."

Rory responded with a tight nod, an unspoken promise passing between them. He closed the door behind him as Jaxson exited, then stood there for a moment, seemingly hesitant, caught between his desire to approach and a fear of causing her further pain.

"You can come closer," Kimber urged gently, patting the bed beside her. "I won't break."

With each tentative step Rory took toward her, Kimber's heart beat a little faster. His face was etched with a look of guilt, adding to the emotional intensity of the moment. She tried to shift herself to sit up more comfortably, causing her to wince at the movement. Rory instantly sprang into action, his concern overriding his previous hesitation.

"Let me help you," he offered, his voice laced with care.

As Rory leaned over her to adjust the pillows, Kimber seized the moment. Reaching up, she grasped his neck, pulling him closer.

"Rory," she whispered, infusing his name with an emotional depth that spoke volumes.

That single utterance, loaded with meaning, seemed to unlock something within Rory. His eyes, dark and intense, met hers, acknowledging the gravity of the moment. Kimber's gaze drifted to his lips, the unspoken longing between them palpable.

"Kimber." Rory's voice was a low growl, charged with emotion as he leaned in, his lips meeting hers in a kiss that felt like destiny.

The kiss ignited between them like a cascade of sparks, a convergence of pent-up emotions and unsaid words. Time seemed to suspend as Rory's tongue traced the seam of her lips, seeking permission, which Kimber eagerly granted. As they deepened their kiss, the world around them faded into insignificance, leaving only the two of them lost in a connection that transcended words, a reaffirmation of their bond that was as deep as it was passionate. At that moment, nothing else mattered but the undeniable truth that they belonged to each other.

When he finally pulled back, Kimber's smile was a soft beacon in the dim room as he settled beside her on the bed.

"I didn't come in here for that," he murmured, his voice a gentle caress. Tenderly, he brushed a stray lock of hair from her forehead, his palm cradling her face like something precious. His thumb traced the smooth flesh of her cheek as he smiled.

"I know. But Rory, there's something I need to say to you," she began, her eyes glistening with tears.

He silenced her with a gentle press of his finger against her lips, a soft but firm gesture.

"Let me go first," he insisted, his eyes locking onto hers with an intensity that spoke volumes. Lowering his hand, he intertwined his fingers with hers. He squeezed her hand, his grip conveying their connection and the undercurrent of vulnerability. "My life… it's been a series of losses. As a Navy SEAL, I've witnessed the end of so many brave lives. And when I left, I wanted something different, a new purpose. That path took me to Los Angeles, where I joined a firm that protected the wealthy. But that job… it was harder than any battlefield I'd faced." He paused, his gaze distant, as if reliving the memories.

"You see, my twin sister, Roslyn, she was this incredible force in fashion. Everyone believed she'd make it big, especially when a Hollywood actress showed interest in her work. But it was all a sham. Roslyn was left with nothing, and it… it nearly destroyed her. She chose not to fight back because the woman responsible was too powerful, too rich. Roslyn hid her pain, but inside, she was crumbling, spiraling into a dark void. The day she tried to end her pain was the day I realized I needed to be there for her. Being so far away, unable to help, made me lose my focus. When the time came to re-enlist, I walked away. I know my view of the wealthy has been clouded by this one incident, but being a body-guard to them only reinforced my beliefs."

"Rory, I—" Kimber started, her voice a whisper of concern.

He gently pressed his finger to her lips again, silencing her with a tender gesture.

"I know, Kimber. You're nothing like them. And I'm ashamed to admit that it took almost losing you on that stage to realize what I was risking. No, that's not entirely true. The moment you stood there, revealing your true self to the world, I knew I'd been wrong to judge you by the actions of others. You're different, Kimber. You have this light in you that brightens everything around you. You give of yourself so freely, so selflessly. I saw it with Chloe, how you protected and comforted her. I love you, Kimber. It's sudden, I know, but it's the truth. I don't deserve it, but I'm asking you—no, begging you—to give me a chance to prove myself to you."

The tears that Kimber had fought so valiantly to hold back now traced silver paths down her cheeks, a silent testament to the depth of her emotions. Rory cradled her face gently in his hands, his thumbs tenderly wiping away each tear that escaped.

"Baby, don't cry," he whispered, his voice a soothing balm. He leaned in, pressing a soft kiss to one tear-stained cheek, then mirrored the gesture on the other. "I didn't mean to bring you to tears."

"I'm not sad, Rory," Kimber replied, her voice shaking with a mixture of emotions. He pulled back slightly, his gaze intense and unwavering as she spoke the truth. "You're the reason I emerged from my shell. I wanted you to see me—the real me. That song… it was my heart speaking directly to you. I am in love with you, too, Rory. You see, beyond my façade to the raw and real imperfections, the scars left by a world that almost broke me. In your eyes, I am truly Kimber. With you, I can embrace love and be loved in return."

Their lips met in a kiss that was more than just a meeting of mouths—it was a profound promise, a silent vow carrying the weight of their love.

"Marry me," Rory murmured against her lips, his words laced with an earnest plea. "Say you'll be mine forever, Kimber. I can't bear the thought of a life without you in it."

He pulled back, his chestnut eyes piercing into hers, searching, hoping to find a reflection of his own deep love. In response, she nodded, her voice barely a whisper. "Yes." Rory enveloped her in his arms, his head resting in the crook of her neck, a silent symbol of their union.

The moment was interrupted by Jaxson's voice. "I take it you two worked things out," he said, a hint of amusement in his tone.

Rory shifted, his demeanor changing as he faced Kimber's brother. "I should have asked you first," he confessed. "I asked her to marry me."

"Good," Jaxson replied with a smile, a brotherly approval in his eyes. "I would have kicked your ass if you hadn't."

Kimber, caught off guard, glanced between the two men, the only ones she'd ever loved. "You're not mad?" she asked, a mix of surprise and relief in her voice.

Jaxson raised his hand in a gesture of peace. "I don't need the details of what goes on between you two, but my best friend and my sister together… it makes sense. But I have to ask… are you going to live at the compound with Kimber?"

"Compound?" Kimber echoed, a hint of confusion in her voice.

Rory's face flushed with embarrassment. "Uh… I don't actually have a house of my own being built. I live in the employee dorms at LTI," he admitted sheepishly.

"I see," Kimber said, narrowing her eyes playfully. "That makes sense, I suppose."

Jaxson, ever the problem solver, grinned. "Well, I think I have a solution."

EPILOGUE

ATLAS STOOD SLIGHTLY APART from the festivities, his gaze pensive as he observed the joyous celebration of Rory and Kimber's wedding. The event had come together quickly, just three months after Kimber's harrowing experience, and now they were blissfully united in matrimony. The ceremony, intimate and heartfelt, took place on the expansive property Kimber shared with her brother, Jaxson. While their own home was in the final stages of construction, Rory and Kimber had made their temporary nest in the house where Kimber and Jaxson had spent their childhood.

Beside him, his dog, Zeus, enjoyed the attention as Atlas absent-mindedly scratched behind his ear. They were on the outskirts of the gathering, watching the newlyweds cut their wedding cake, a symbol of their sweet future together. Atlas' eyes, however, roamed the crowd, not seeking his team members but searching for one person in particular. *Her*.

Taylor Davis, the baker, the woman who inexplicably captivated his thoughts. Despite his best efforts to resist, he found himself ensnared by the memory of a fleeting moment they shared, a moment so potent that the taste of her skin still lingered on his lips. Since that encounter, no one else had come close to stirring such feelings within him. She had unintentionally ruined him for anyone else.

His brooding was interrupted by Luca Cashen, the team's medic, who slid into the chair beside him.

"How's it hanging, boss?" Luca inquired with a casualness that belied his observation.

Atlas shot back with a wry retort, "Why? You worried about my dick, Cashen?"

Zeus barked as if in agreement with his owner.

"Whoa there…" Luca, hands raised in mock surrender, chuckled. "Just a figure of speech, boss. You seem a bit off lately, just checking if you're good."

Atlas ran a hand down his face, the weight of his thoughts momentarily visible. "Yeah… good. Just busy with business and trying to expand the team. With Apollo away again, there's a lot to handle."

Luca nodded, understanding the burden of leadership. As Atlas was about to continue, his attention was suddenly captured by Creed, another team member, engaging in conversation with Taylor. A low growl escaped Atlas, much to Luca's amusement.

"Ah… I see what's up now," Luca said with a knowing grin.

Atlas glared at him. "See what?"

"A woman has you all twisted up. And look, Creed is making his move. You just gonna sit there?"

"Fuck, no," Atlas declared, standing abruptly. "Zeus, let's go." With a pat on his leg, he signaled the dog to follow.

As he began to approach her, his progress was halted by Jaxson tapping a knife against his glass, calling for everyone's attention. Atlas stopped, his focus torn between Taylor and the unfolding scene. Taylor stood alone now, her face etched with an emotion Atlas couldn't quite decipher, as Creed had drifted toward the makeshift bar.

Jaxson, with a wide smile, pulled Kimber into his embrace.

"Thank you all for joining us today. I'm the luckiest man alive to have married this incredible woman," he said, his voice filled with warmth and affection. The crowd responded with cheers and whistles.

"And though she has way more than I can ever give her in return… I wanted to try."

Everyone laughed. They knew Rory was referring to the fact that his wife was loaded. Her records still made money, and since her concert, where she'd revealed herself to her fans, they'd tripled in revenue.

As Jaxson continued, Atlas' attention wavered. He was more aware of the way Taylor's gaze lingered on the happy couple, a mix of emotions playing across her features. His thoughts were also on Rory and Kimber's evolving life, their music career taking a new turn with their band, Revived, and their agreement to work part-time, allowing Rory to travel with Kimber.

Atlas watched as Rory turned Kimber around. Jaxson and Davis had somehow moved a trailer into the backyard. On top was a tarp.

"Kimber, I made a promise to you a while back. And I know you've probably forgotten, but I didn't." He led her to where her brother stood. "It took some time, but I made it work. Go on, baby. Look."

Jaxson's voice brought Atlas back to the moment. He watched as Kimber was led to a surprise—a beautifully crafted piano hidden under a tarp. Her reaction was one of pure joy and disbelief.

Turning away from the touching scene, Atlas and Zeus made their way to the now deserted bar. He reached over the counter and grabbed a beer, seeking the cold comfort it offered.

"Pretty sure that's stealing," a familiar voice teased from behind him.

The sound of her voice was like a spark igniting dry tinder, sending a rush of heat through him. "Is it stealing if it's all paid for?"

She shrugged, her face a mask of unsure emotions. Taylor grabbed a glass from the tiny bar and turned away from him.

"Hey, wait a second."

Zeus, recognizing the sweet scent that always seemed to cover her skin, brushed against her. Taylor reached down and rubbed his head.

"Hey, boy. Haven't seen you around." Her eyes lifted to meet his.

"I've been staying away like you asked—that means him, too." Atlas rolled his shoulders, trying to make the prickling sensations stop.

"Right." She wiped her hand down her pant leg. "I've got to go. I need to cut the rest of the cake for the guests."

She started to step away, but Atlas reached out and grabbed her arm. "Wait."

Taylor stopped and sighed. "Atlas." Her voice was a whisper—a sound that went straight to his groin. "Please… I told you."

"I know." He cut her off. "But I want to know why. What we shared was more than pent-up frustration, Taylor. You know it. I know it. So give me one good reason we can't explore the heat we have."

Taylor shook her head. "What we had… was nothing more than two people blowing off steam. If your dog hadn't been stealing my damn cupcakes, we'd never have met up like that."

"You know that's not true."

The memory of her at the bar washed over him. She'd been in her wedding dress, sitting on a stool. When he approached her that night to make sure she was ok, her fiery response knocked him on his ass. She sparked something in him that night that he couldn't forget—and when Zeus had been caught sneaking into the back of her bakery, he knew fate was intervening. But she'd been hurt and had a wall around her bigger than the Great Wall of China. It was going to take a strong man to scale it.

Atlas stood there, a man torn by the conflicting emotions and the undeniable pull he felt toward Taylor. He was well aware that the sensible thing to do would be to walk away. Hell, he was no stranger to hardship and loss; his last mission with his SEAL team had been a brutal reminder of that. The only solace in those dark times had been Zeus, the loyal dog who now lavished affection on the very woman who had unwittingly trapped his thoughts. Zeus was more than just a companion. He was a living link to Atlas' fallen comrade, Mark, and now a vital part of his life.

Taylor's sudden withdrawal, jerking her arm from his grasp and stepping back, only heightened the tension between them. Her eyes met his, a turbulent mix of desire and sadness swirling in their depths, striking Atlas with the force of a physical blow.

"I can't lose focus. The bakery is all I have, Atlas. I let one man nearly destroy me. I won't make that mistake again. No matter how much I might want to," she declared, her words slicing through the air between them.

Her departure left an intense void, her words echoing in his mind like a haunting refrain. She wanted him, that much was clear, but fear held her back. Atlas wasn't sure he had the energy to delve into the depths of that fear, to unearth what lay beneath.

With a heavy heart, he turned toward the front of the house, Zeus trailing closely behind. The dog's soft whimper made him glance down.

"I know, buddy. She doesn't want us," he murmured, more to himself than to Zeus.

Zeus paused, glancing back and prompting Atlas to follow his gaze. His heart skipped a beat at the sight of Taylor alone and leaning against a tree. Her body language spoke of tension, and he didn't miss the subtle tremors that shook her frame. When she caught his gaze and quickly composed herself, the realization that she had been crying struck him hard.

Atlas halted, a wave of emotions raging within him. Her words said one thing, but her body, her tears, told a different story. He wanted to uncover the secrets she held so closely, to understand the enigma of her words and actions.

Despite his own brokenness, Atlas was not one to give up easily. He could sense the battle ahead, the resistance she was putting up, yet he couldn't ignore the powerful connection they shared, a bond that seemed to weave around them, defying her attempts to sever it. She represented a challenge like no other, a battle he was unwittingly prepared to fight.

Taylor might be running from what they shared, but Atlas was ready to wait, to watch, to understand. He knew the connection they had felt was real, as tangible as the thread that seemed to bind them together.

Yes, Atlas was broken, but he was not defeated. He knew the road ahead would be the toughest he'd ever faced, but he was ready. With Zeus at his side, he was prepared to traverse the complicated terrain.

"Come on, Zeus. We need a plan."

After a painful breakup, Taylor wants a simple life, avoiding complex figures like Atlas Lyons, the charismatic ex-Navy SEAL.

His mischievous dog, a cupcake heist, and a night she can't seem to erase from her thoughts—despite her resolve to stay detached.

When Taylor faces danger linked to her past, Atlas becomes her protector, showing he's willing to face any threat for her.

Their bond tests whether Atlas can not only protect Taylor but also win her heart, proving they can face any challenge together.

Find out in Protecting Taylor: Team Atlas Book Two

Sign up for the Alpha Book Boyfriend Newsletter and get a coupon for a FREE Novella.
Then, use it to read Protecting Avery

ABOUT LC

"Tattoos, whiskey, and bullets—where passion meets protection."

An International and USA Today Bestselling author, LC's an unapologetic down-home southern gal—with a bit of a dirty mouth who bleeds red, white, and blue. LC's never met a brooding hero she didn't love. She writes her men cut, tattooed, and tender for their down but not out ladies who need a little love from the right man. Her alpha heroes are less shades of gray and more shades of blue.

When she's not writing her hunky heroes, creating swoon-worthy love connections—you'll find LC curled up on the couch with a glass of peach crown and her very own sexy tattooed cop watching true crime on the television.

www.AuthorLCTaylor.com